MONUMENT

Monument

And Other Stories

David Milofsky

Also By David Milofsky

Scare Tactics

A Message from Carnegie

A Milwaukee Inheritance

Where I'm Living Now (stories)

A Friend of Kissinger

Eternal People

Color of Law

Playing From Memory

These stories appeared in slightly different form in the following magazines:

Prairie Schooner
The Bellevue Literary Review
The South Dakota Review
Denver Quarterly
Beloit Fiction Journal
TriQuartely
"Erev" was included in *Best Stories of the Bellevue Literary Review* and received special mention in the Pushcart Prize 2011.

CONTENTS

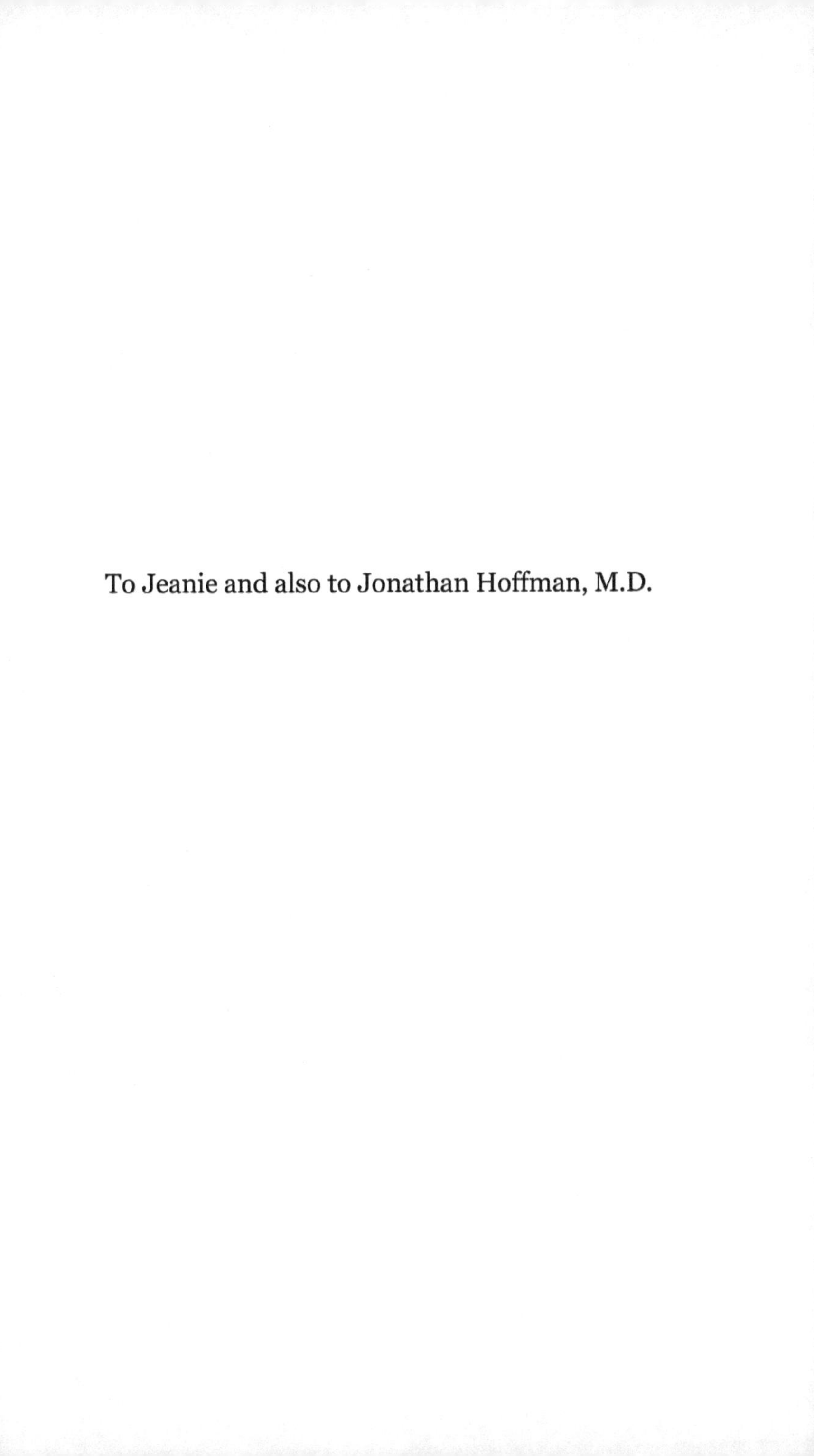

To Jeanie and also to Jonathan Hoffman, M.D.

"Nothing happens in the suburbs."
—Walter Garnsey, in conversation

"Have you ever lived in the suburbs? It's sterile. It's
nothing. It's wasting your life."
—Ed Koch, Mayor of New York City

MONUMENT

A nurse looked disapprovingly at Pavel Rosen as she walked by, her stockings scratching a threnody beneath her starched skirt. Charlie could understand. Pavel was never neat, but today he wore army fatigues that were caked with clay and a tattered green lumber jacket. His hair was hanging in his face, and he was smiling manically, displaying gapped yellow teeth and swollen gums. "What was that, Pavel?" Charlie said. "I didn't hear you"

Pavel didn't seem to mind Charlie's inattention. "This place is crazy," he said. "They weren't going to let me up here until I told them I was a relative. I'm too old to be your brother, not old enough to be your father. I said I was your uncle." Now he indicated the closed door behind them. "Your mother, does she have a brother?" He seemed anxious lest his lie offend.

"She did," Charlie said. "But he died a few years ago. It's okay, they weren't close. I think she'd rather have you as a brother, to tell the truth."

Pavel smiled broadly as this. "I like her very much," he said. His v's were w's and a wave of fatigue swept over Charlie. He had been doing sentry duty for six hours. Now that he had put Hannah in the hospice, announcing if not her imminent death, then its likelihood, the stream of visitors had been unending. Colleagues, students, friends, acquaintances, even a newspaper reporter eager to get the jump on her obituary, had all come by asking to see her. They came at all hours, not even waiting in the small anteroom across the hall until someone came out, but simply walking in, putting the flowers on the table, and joining whatever conversation was in progress.

In a way this was as it should be because this was the way his mother had lived; her house and office were open to anyone who wanted to drop by, no regular hours. Now, in her last days Hannah's hair looked like that of an empress, her arms reaching out blindly to hold the proffered hands of the faithful, giving them her blessing as they gave her theirs, allowing the mourners one last kiss before death.

Finally, it had become necessary to set some limit on the horde of visitors to allow her to rest. The doctor had threatened to restrict visits and allow only family members in the room, but threats had never had much effect on Hannah. She fixed him with a cold stare and said she'd leave if he tried to put limits on her social life. She wanted to see people, she said. What else did she have left? The compromise was for Charlie to stand guard. Now he looked at Pavel, whom he hardly knew, and wondered why any of them had come.

"There's someone with her right now," Charlie said. "You want to wait? Too many people at once tire her out."

Pavel's smile was replaced by a look of painted recognition. "I know," he said. "My father, the same. Five years."

Charlie vaguely remembered Hannah telling him when Pavel was hired, how excited she had been. "He's a real artist," she said. "From New York, but he's European, I think. All he cares about is art. He'll never last in Milwaukee."

Yet he had, at least he was still here, in the hall in his baggy pants, sharing confidences. "I'm sorry," was all Charlie could think of to say.

Pavel nodded. "He was a little man, a shoemaker, but he had a good strong face, sensitive. I can show, in my studio."

"Your studio?" Charlie said dumbly.

"Yes, of course. I made a cast before he died. Every day before I work, I see Papa. Now I do Hannah."

Despite himself, Charlie smiled. "You want to make a statue of my mother?"

"No, not the legs, the body. Just her head, that is most important. Your mother is a great woman, you know. She belongs not just to you but to everyone." Then, as if he thought he might have insulted Charlie, Pavel patted his arm. "Did I say wrong? She is your Mama, of course that we know. But we all love her too, you see? And she has such a wonderful forehead." Pavel gazed into space, lost in the image, while Charlie tried to remember what Hannah's forehead looked like.

"I waited," Pavel continued, "because I thought maybe she will get well. But now I must work fast. You see?" Without waiting for an answer, he grabbed Charlie's arm and started pulling him down the hall.

"Pavel, wait a minute. I've got to watch the door."

"It is okay," Pavel called over his shoulder. "The nurse she will do it for you. Come."

Outside, Pavel had parked his van in a doctor's parking space. By the time Charlie got downstairs, he and a boy were loading boxes of clay onto a hospital cart marked "Surgery." Charlie started to protest, but Pavel handed him a box. "Here," he said with authority. "They tow the car away soon."

Together they loaded four boxes of clay, a potter's wheel, some knives and an apron onto the cart. Then Pavel pulled a sketch pad and a box of paints out of the back seat. Charlie remembered one of the objections to hiring Pavel had been that he painted his sculptures, feeling dissatisfied with the sameness of gray. Now Pavel turned and kissed the boy who then drove off. "My son," he said.

"Pavel, how are we going to get all this stuff upstairs?"

Pavel looked up at the imposing building, at the statue of the Virgin Mary that watched over the entrance, and then at Charlie. "We take the elevator," he said decisively.

When Charlie opened Hannah's door, a shot of eucalyptus hit him from the vaporized air and made him choke. The rooms in the hospice were supposed to make the patients feel at home, but immediately upon arriving, Hannah had ordered everything to be changed. The sofa and chairs were covered with Indian bedspreads; the pictures on the wall had been replaced by Matisse reproductions; two of Hannah's vases were on the end table; and a portable phonograph played Schonberg.

Two women were with her when Charlie and Pavel wheeled the cart into the room, but they showed no sign of recognition. Introductions were apparently not in order. One sat with her legs crossed, holding Hannah's hand while the other, whom Charlie now remembered was a yoga instructor, seemed in the middle of some complex exercise with her right leg. For a moment, he hesitated before approaching the bed. He had never felt at ease with some of his mother's friends. "Mom?" he said at last.

Her head moved but her body, regal in a blue embroidered nightgown, seemed ethereal, unattached to anything. Only her eyes, large and sad, indicated she had heard. Now her cracked lips moved. "Kiss me," she said.

Charlie bent and brushed her cheek, feeling its paper thinness and wondering why it was so cold. He tried hard not to think about it. "Pavel's here to see you."

Hannah seemed rejuvenated by this. Her eyes opened wide now, and she tried to smile. "Pa..l," she said, and held out her free hand in what she imagined was his direction.

Pavel took it and kissed it like a cavalier. "Pavel wants to do your head,": Charlie said, realizing how odd this sounded. He expected her to laugh and knew it was because he wanted her to, to see her eyes dance and her mouth transformed again. But Hannah was perfectly sober, though Charlie thought she was pleased. Her eyes turned to Pavel, waiting for an explanation.

"It would be beautiful, Hannah," he said. "Always, I admire your forehead, like a great ship going to sea, I think. It moves me."

Hannah said nothing and Charlie thought he saw a hint of amusement in her expression. Then she pointed to the foot of her bed, between the silent woman and the yoga instructor. Pavel looked questioningly at Charlie.

"I think she wants you to get to work," he said.

"Ja, ja, I start then," Pavel said. "Right now, I start."

Charlie watched him for a while, but then he remembered he was supposed to be outside. When he opened the door, a nurse was staring at him. She wore her hair in a severe bun with a starched cap pinned to it and seemed about to speak. Some of the younger nurses wore street clothes, but Charlie could see this one was a traditionalist. He started to get out of her way, assuming she had to do something to Hannah, but she didn't move. "Doctor wants to see you" she said, her lips barely moving.

Then she was walking back down the hall.

In the lounge, three nurses were watching a doctor show on television. They drank coke and tried to guess the diagnosis of a huge pregnant woman who was heaving up and down on an examining table like a fish on a pier.

"Maybe she's epileptic," the first nurse said. "My sister had it and she'd get like that sometimes."

"She's pregnant."

"So? You can be pregnant and epileptic too, can't you?"

"How about the hypertension then?" the second nurse put in.

"Epileptics get that. It's all over the place now," the first nurse insisted.

"Sure, I just don't see why she has to be epileptic. Christ, you'd think it was the only disease in the world."

"It's not a disease," the first nurse said.

"I know that. Jesus."

The doctor came in to end the debate, and nurses grudgingly drank their cokes and left. No one turned the set off, however, and now there were all these little televisions in the operating room going "beep, beep," while people in white yelled "stat" at each other and rushed around. The pregnant woman seemed alone, totally ignored, even though she was still throwing herself on and off the table at regular intervals.

When the doctor came over Charlie was tempted to ask him what he thought the woman's problem was, but the man didn't seem interested. He was tall and ascetic-looking, as if he'd lived a life of denial, and wore a red jogging suit. Charlie wondered if he had interrupted the doctor's' workout or if he always dressed this way. He didn't look like the doctors on the television show, but then the hospice wasn't much like that hospital either. Everything here was very calm. No one yelled anything and people were dying all the time. As he walked up and down the halls, Charlie looked into their empty rooms and wondered about the lives they had lived. "Mr. Fuller?" the doctor said now and extended his hand. "I'm Dr. Evens."

Charlie tried to stand as much to get on equal ground as out of courtesy. But the chair held him in its grasp, so he shook hands sitting down. He thought the doctor looked worried or maybe it was only that his feet hurt from the jogging. Now he sat, though the nurse remained standing at his side, like a sentry. She shook a cigarette from a pack of Kents, lit it, and blew smoke at the ceiling.

"Are you Mrs. Fuller's only relative? The doctor asked.

"Her husband's dead," Charlie said. The man was Hannah's second husband, not Charlie's father, and they had never gotten along. Two years ago, when Hannah got sick, he just disappeared, didn't want to be bothered, Charlie thought. But Hannah had given him the benefit of the doubt. "Death bothers people," she had written. "I hope my death won't bother you too much. I want to see you, spend time with you while I'm still here. Don't stay away." So, Charlie came, but he never forgave Hannah's husband, and he was glad she'd never taken the man's name. As far as Charlie was concerned, he was dead.

"And you're Mrs. Fuller's only child?"

"I'm it," Charlie said.

The doctor nodded and looked at the floor. "Your mother's a very well-known woman," he began, just to say something, Charlie thought. Hannah had done well, considering she hadn't started until she was nearly forty. But no one had heard of her outside the Midwest. He doubted the doctor even knew what she did.

"She's a painter," Charlie said, to help the conversation along.

"Yes," the doctor said gratefully. "Actually, I saw her show last year at the art center, the retrospective. And a professor, too, I believe?"

Hannah was only an associate at the Extension. But Charlie didn't say anything. She should have been a professor by now. Let the doctor think she was, what harm could that do?

Dr Evans moved his chair closer, as if to invite confidence, but the nurse loomed over his shoulder like a mountain. They weren't going to keep anything from her. "Mr. Fuller," the doctor said in a hushed voice. "We have a little problem." He looked up at the nurse, who nodded in agreement.

"You mean the visitors?" I've been standing at the door all morning. Two at a time, just like you said."

The nurse snorted at this and spoke for the first time. "Two at a time maybe, but she takes down all her pictures, won't take a bath, don't take her pills and they're' doing exercises in there and her dying."

The doctor held up his hand for peace. "Mr. Fuller, the nurses are concerned because Mrs., that is, Professor Fuller, won't take her medication."

"She says it makes her feel vague," Charlie said.

"Vague?"

"Doped up, out of it," Charlie searched for other synonyms but could think of none. "She doesn't like feeling that way; she wants to be sharp, alive while she still is."

"Ah," the doctor said and nodded. "Our policy here is that patients should be pain-free," he said mildly.

"It's her pain, right" Charlie replied.

"Indeed," the doctor agreed. "That's true."

The nurse sat down now and put on a reasonable face. "I'm sure your mother must be a very nice person to have so many friends," she began, but her expression made Charlie feel she thought no such thing. In fact, he wouldn't have described Hannah as nice himself. It didn't really surprise him that the nurses should have trouble handling her; he just didn't know what to do about it.

"Well," the nurse continued, "we've never had a patient with so many visitors, never had this problem before. Usually, folks won't come. But when your mother snaps, it bothers some of the younger girls."

Charlie doubted this. Nothing seemed to bother the young nurses who chewed gum noisily and walked the halls with an insouciance that came, he guessed, from a premature familiarity with death. "She's dying," he said. "She knows it and she doesn't like it and to tell you the truth, she always did have a temper. She says no one here knows how to give her a bath without it hurting. I guess you'll just have to get used to her. One thing, she doesn't like everybody calling her by her first name."

The nurse's mouth opened fast, like she was going to say something, but then shut tight. Charlie could see she was mad, but he didn't care. "We encourage informality her," the doctor said. "Everyone's on a first-name basis."

"I don't hear anyone calling you by your first name," Charlie said.

"That's different," the doctor said.

Charlie nodded. This was bullshit but he didn't want to argue about it. The room seemed hot and close, and he wondered how Pavel was doing. "Is that all?"

"Well, there is one thing. Apparently, there's a workman in your mother's room with Mrs. Fuller."

"He's an artist," Charlie said. "A professor, too."

"Ah," the doctor said, impressed. "It's just that the nurses are worried about the sanitary conditions."

Charlie looked at the doctor with his jogging suit and concerned expression. To hear him tell it, he never worried about a thing. It was always the nurses. But he had a lot of forehead bisected by thick furrows. Probably he worked hard for his money and didn't need difficult patients on top of it. It wasn't really his fault. "She's got cancer and what, a week, maybe two, to live."

The doctor lowered his head in assent but said nothing. Predictions were not his game; they could get him in trouble if he was wrong.

"What's the worst thing that could happen? She might get an infection and die a day or two earlier, but at least she'd be happy because she got to see her friends. To tell the truth, I don't care if she has a bath for the rest of her life. Even if I did, she'd do what she wants. And the artist stays."

The doctor shrugged and left the room, followed by the nurse. Charlie got a coke and went outside to drink it. He wanted to rid himself of the stuffy feeling in his head and figured the nurses could handle visitors for a while. A freighter was moving toward the harbor out on the lake, and as he watched its slow progression, Charlie thought of what Pavel had said about Hannah's head and he felt bad that he hadn't talked to her more. Usually, he'd go in and sit next to her bed at night and hold her hand. When he would finally get up to leave at two or three, she would turn to him, fear in her eyes, as if death would ambush her in his absence. So, Charlie would sit down again and wait for her to sleep. If she didn't doze off, he would stay in the chair all night, stroking her forearm, staring into the blackness, waiting for the lake to turn blue.

It reminded him of the time he'd gotten pneumonia and Hannah didn't move from his bedside for a week. Not that he thought of this as payback, but he was glad he was there, happy that he could do something for her others couldn't. He and Hannah had not been close since he dropped out of graduate school and now, he realized that when she died, he would be alone in an entirely new way. He wasn't looking forward to that.

Upstairs, Pavel had spread out his things on every available surface. Boxes of clay lay on the windowsill and on the floor and a huge mound sat on a board atop the hospital cart at the foot of the bed. Pavel sat staring at Hannah, who ignored him, deep within herself. The silent woman had gone now but the yoga instructor was still there, holding Hannah's hand. At first, it seemed odd that no one said anything, that this wasn't a more social occasion, but then he remembered asking Hannah how she felt about her subject when she did portraits, whether it mattered to her if the people started to sweat or seemed uncomfortable in their poses. "I never think about it," she said. "I never even offer them a glass of water. To me, they're just like pieces of fruit for a still-life."

Pavel began to draw, but when Charlie peered over his shoulder, it didn't look like anything: a tangle of black lines with shadowing in between. This was going to be some sculpture, he decided, and went outside.

Around six, the doctor showed up while Charlie was drinking coffee in the group kitchen. All the dying people were supposed to gather here and eat macaroni and cheese while they comforted each other. But except for the picture in the brochure they handed him when Hannah checked in, Charlie had never seen anyone in the kitchen besides a black orderly who said, "What's happening?" and a man who looked like a minister from one of the more liberal protestant denominations. A Congregationalist, maybe, or a Unitarian. "May I?" the doctor asked, pointing to a chair.

"Help yourself," Charlie said, indicating the coffee pot, but the doctor just smiled and folded his hands on the table as if he was going to say grace.

"Are you a professor, too, Mr. Fuller?"

Charlie felt himself flush, though he knew the man was just being polite. It was a natural question. Doctor's' sons became doctors. "I work in a department store," he said, keeping it simple. He could have told him he was assistant manager, which happened to be true, but being the manager of a catalogue outlet in Fort Wayne was not going to impress anyone. And why should the doctor care? Now Charlie realized it didn't matter as much to him anymore. Once Hannah was gone there would be no one with high expectations for him, no one to push against, to disappoint, not even himself.

"Here in town.?"

"No, down in Indiana, Fort Wayne." He had always liked the name, which was why he'd gone there in the first place, and Wanda. And now that Wanda had gone it was the only reason he stayed. He had always imagined a garrison with men in tri-corner hats fighting off the Indians despite incredible hardships. But little of Fort Wayne's heroic heritage remained, as far as Charlie could tell. The closest he'd come to seeing it was during the big flood in '91 when he looked out his kitchen window and saw his car floating down the driveway toward the street. It was exciting, but saving an old Chevy from drowning was not the same as fighting for your life.

"Must be tough on your family having you all the way up here."

Charlie didn't correct the doctor about the family. "I guess it's tougher on her," he said, nodding at Hannah's door.

"Of course," said Dr. Evans. "Shall we have a look?"

Charlie rinsed his cup in the sink, and they crossed the hall together. The yoga instructor was gone and now there were only Hannah and Pavel facing each other mutely. The boxes of clay were empty and the mound on the platform had metamorphosed, taking on both shape and form as Pavel attacked it with his knife. There was a bowl of water on the table and every so often he would slap some of it on the clay and smooth it lovingly with his fingers.

Hannah's head barely dented the large pillow, and her eyes were closed. She lay not moving but with her right hand extended as if she was making a point in an argument. For a moment Charlie considered introducing Pavel and the doctor but then decided against it. Instead, he walked around behind Pavel and looked past the artist at his mother.

It was remarkable. Her hollowed cheeks had gained substance in the clay; her staring eyes were still, pained but lucid; her thin lips and sharp chin were there too, and the forehead Pavel said looked like a ship's prow had successfully been rendered, as if life had been removed from Hannah's frail body through Pavel's hand and then grafted onto the bust. Her mouth was slightly agape, and

Charlie could see her lower lip, as if she was baring her teeth at someone. But anger was all right, he thought; anger was fine. He liked to think of her that way.

Looking at the two Hannahs, Charlie remembered the professor in the only art history course had he had taken in college. The man would stalk around the podium in the lecture hall with a long pointer in his hand, occasionally turning to jab at a slide of a Giotto or Cimabue. His constant remark, or perhaps it was just the only one Charlie remembered, was "Monumental." Everything was monumental, everything good, that is. Charlie had told Hannah, who smiled but said nothing. Now he thought he saw what the professor meant. Pavel's bust was monumental, too, larger than life, though it had life in it. Hannah's life. It suggested her, the best and toughest things about her, without being her, or, Charlie knew, replacing her. It was something.

Pavel stood up and squared his shoulders. As if on cue, the doctor moved to the bed and put his fingers on Hannah's wrist. Then he ran his palm delicately across her face, though her eyes were already shut. She had died, Charlie realized, while he was thinking about the bust. It made him feel disloyal.

"Time of death, 7:17," the doctor said quietly.

For a few minutes, no one said anything. Finally, the doctor pressed the call button on the wall. In the moment before the nurses came in, Charlie tried to memorize the scene, to place them all forever in time. The doctor with his faint, embarrassed smile; the two Hannahs mimicking one another; Pavel. He looked at the artist and saw his eyes were shining and Charlie realized he was crying too, that water was running down his face and onto his shirt front.

They stood there, facing each other, crying separately. Then Charlie reached out and pulled Pavel close, smelling the smaller man but not caring and not caring either when the nurses came in and saw two men embracing in a house of death.

The doctor walked over and patted Charlie on the shoulder. Without saying anything, Charlie knew he wanted them to leave. There were things to be done, things Charlie wouldn't want to see, though of course they would understand if he would like a few moments alone with his mother.

Charlie looked at Hannah. She already seemed to be losing color, becoming translucent, her skin closer now to the light blue of the nightgown than to its normal color. He couldn't think what he would say to her corpse that he hadn't been able to say while she was alive, but silence made him feel inadequate. He shook his head. "So that's it?" he said at last. "That's all there is to it?"

The doctor smiled ruefully. "I'm afraid so. At least it was peaceful."

Charlie nodded. Then he put his arm around Pavel's shoulders and together they walked out the door.

LITTLE VIRTUES, LITTLE VICES

My wife handed me the phone with a grimace that said everything, but just in case I hadn't understood, she said, "It's him again. Your friend." I had more than one friend, but I knew who she meant and, in that moment, regretted the coming argument that would ruin the evening. I took the receiver from her and heard Risto Lannell's high-pitched voice laughing into the phone.

"Risto," I said. "Where are you?"

The laughter disappeared now, replaced by a bluff air of insult.

"Where am I? I thought you might ask how I am."

"I know how you are," I said. "But if you want me to come and get you, I need directions."

Risto grunted into the phone. "You'll have to ask my friend." I waited and the bartender came on the line. The man didn't sound embarrassed, just bored.

"Your buddy's at the Depot Tavern, across from the old train station on East Washington, and he owes me fifteen bucks."

"I'll be there in ten minutes," I said.

My wife had remained standing throughout the call, but now she put the pot roast on the table and placed her hands on her hips. "Who elected you?"

"Pardon?" I was eating the pot roast, trying to ignore the fact that she'd prepared a special dinner, put the kid to bed early, the closest we'd had to a celebration in months. Not that there was anything in particular to celebrate, but we were trying. We were good at trying, or at least we always had been.

"You know what I mean," she continued. "Doesn't Risto have anyone else who could drive him home when he gets drunk? What about his wife?"

The question made me uncomfortable because I knew that despite the surface irritation, I wanted Risto to call me. I wanted to be crucial, the one he could count on when everyone else was gone. I had no real complaints with my life, or at least I thought I had no right to complain. But more and more a grinding regularity had taken over. I knew at the beginning of every day what would happen and went to bed at night without having surprised myself. When I was eighteen, I hitched across the country with a friend, scaring the hell out of our parents. Now I imagined taking off with Risto, riding the rails, sharing a bottle of rotgut with whoever happened to be in our boxcar. Picking him up at a tavern and driving him home twice a week wasn't the same, but it was as close as I was likely to come these days. It was depressing to think how little it took to make my life seem more exciting, for this was not the way I thought things would be, not the way I'd ever seen myself. "He calls me," I said simply.

"Sure, I get that, but why do you have to go? This is the third time this week. What about us, Tony?"

She was right and I knew my friendship with Risto was a way to avoid facing my disappointment in the marriage. Before the baby, I had imagined that would be the answer, and before that it was my job. Now I was running out of answers, and it was time to give the whole thing some serious thought, but I never considered turning Risto down when he called. It interested me that I had a drunk as a friend; I thought it told me something new about myself. Inclined toward melancholy, Risto rose to eloquence, even poetry, when he was drinking. Enshrined on a tavern stool on a rainy night, he seemed to break through to new truths, though they were evanescent in the light of day. Besides, he was the only person I knew well who didn't work at the University and it was a relief to talk about something besides department politics and tenure decisions. I shoved a potato in my mouth and rose to leave.

"Sorry," I said. "I won't be late."

The Depot turned out to be a hole in the wall six blocks down from the Capitol, whose main virtue as far as I could tell was that it was across the street from the lab where Risto worked as a chemist. In the six months I'd been driving him home, I had watched a descent from the glossy bars on Capitol Square, down State Street, where he mingled with the students, and now over to East Washington. The Depot wasn't much but it was clean and empty. Risto was pressed against a wall in the corner of the room still wearing his coat and hat. I remembered being struck when we first met by the casually elegant way he dressed. His clothes were old but good and his socks always matched. I was surprised when I discovered he wasn't the heir to some immense eastern fortune, but actually a public-school boy like me. Now, with his prim bow tie and green vest he looked more like an accountant who had lost his way. But something of the old Risto remained. His face was fiery red, and his glasses were misted over, but there was an air of dignity about him and his speech was eerily lucid.

"Good to see you," he said, offering his hand as if we were meeting at a Rotary luncheon.

I sat down next to him, and the bartender walked over. He was a thin man with a slight smile on his face. "What'll you have?"

"Nothing for me." Risto held up his glass for a refill, but the bartender ignored him. I put a twenty on the bar and the man went for my change. For a moment, I thought Risto would protest, but then he replaced his glass on the bar with a soft thud. "Time to go," he said.

There was no point in talking to Risto about his drinking. In fact, not talking had a lot to do with our friendship. He already knew everything I'd tell him anyway. He had a nice wife, a son, a good job, and the only explanation he ever offered was his name. "My brother's the same way," he told me once. "Got a last name for a first name. My old man thought he was honoring his mother's family or something, thought it'd give us some class. God knows, it never occurred to him that I'd rather be Fred or Joe, anything rather than fucking Risto." But that was all. The truth was he didn't know why he drank. He didn't even like the taste of whiskey.

Risto lived on the West Side in a small bungalow. When we got there all the lights were on. "Come on in," he said. "For a nightcap."

"I've got work to do," I said, thinking of the pot roast.

"Sure," he said. "But you can do it later; that's the great thing, there's always later. Anyway, Sue'd like to see you."

Risto's wife was waiting at the door when we got there. She was slim, dark and pretty, though it seemed to me she'd aged in the time I'd known her. "Kip in bed?" Risto asked in a jovial voice.

"Yes, thank God." Sue stood in the doorway for a moment as if she was trying to decide whether to let us in.

Then she stepped aside and offered me her cheek. "Nice to see you, Tony. Thanks for bringing him home"

Risto dropped his coat on the floor and walked to the back of the house, leaving Sue and me alone. "Can I get you something?" she said at last. "Coffee? A drink?"

I said yes to give her something to do with her hands and stood in their small living room by myself, waiting. I remembered the first time we met. It was at a party at the Unitarian church and Sue stood out because she was better dressed than the other women. When we were introduced, she took my hand like a man and looked directly into my eyes, as if she was interested and not afraid of seeming so. Then when I thought she'd say something innocuous, she asked, "Who's that guy over there?"

"The one with the English accent? He teaches in the Chemistry Department."

"He sounds like he spent a weekend in London once and has been trying to remember what they sound like ever since."

"I think it's the real thing, kind of. He's from New Zealand, but he's been away for a while."

She nodded then looked back at me. "I don't think there's much of the real thing in this whole damned room." Then she walked away.

I roamed around her living room, picking things up and putting them down, examining by reflex the books on the shelves. There were pictures, of Risto in a tennis sweater on the mantelpiece, much thinner and younger; of the three of them smiling on vacation somewhere in the mountains; several dim, gold-rimmed portraits of relatives. There was a fire in the grate, hooked rugs on the floor; Sue apparently did needlepoint, too. Everything seemed too normal for the tension I felt in this house, but perhaps tension was normal too for some people.

Sue returned with the coffee and put it on the end table next to the couch. "Where's Risto," I asked.

"Asleep," she said contemptuously. "The other night he didn't even get his coat off before he passed out. Then he wakes up in the morning, takes a shower and goes off to work as if nothing happened. At least he's not a sloppy drunk. I don't think he's thrown up in all the time I've known him."

"He's been this way since the beginning?" She looked at me as I'd accused her and I immediately regretted saying anything.

"It's not something you catch suddenly," she said sharply. "It's not like a cold; you don't get over it either." Then, as if she was ashamed of her anger, she took my hand. "I'm sorry."

It didn't bother me. Her anger made me feel important. I sipped the coffee and when I looked back, Sue's eyes were black as pitch. Without saying anything more she cradled my face in her hands and pulled me toward her. I expected an embrace, perhaps some tears, but instead her kiss was passionate, her mouth warm and soft. When I attempted to pull away, she held me tight, and I found that irresistible. The room seemed all wrong for a seduction scene. It was too bright and cozy, and the boy's toys were scattered around from his afternoon's play. "Love me," Sue said. And then in a lower voice, "He won't."

The house was dark when I got home, and my wife had gone to bed. I walked through the downstairs rooms, guiding myself by touch like a blind man. Something about the familiar emptiness was reassuring in the middle of the night. I sat in my old leather chair, then stood up again. In her room, my daughter was asleep, her arms and legs at impossible angles, as if she had been thrown into her crib like a doll and my wife's shallow breaths were audible in the quiet house. Everything seemed the same; the night lulled me. But I still felt Sue's arms around me, smelled her scent, and knew that Risto's proximity, the possibility of disaster had aroused me as much as his wife. And I knew that what I was following was not just Risto's decline but in some peculiar way my own, though at a much different rate. Risto didn't live like the rest of us; he broke all the rules by avoiding responsibility and throwing himself on the mercy of others. While I thought I was rescuing Risto, he seemed to be having more fun. I continually imagined myself in other places, with other women, doing a different job, but Risto was content with things as they were, and this seemed like a gift. There had been a good time for me, then that ended without there seeming to be a transition period. The odd thing was that rather than scaring me, this thought was exciting. Finally, I lay back against the pillows, listening to my wife breathe, feeling her warmth. She reached for me in her sleep, resting her arm on my leg and I started to feel drowsy, but a pulse pounded in my forehead, and it took over an hour to get to sleep.

For the next two weeks, I heard nothing from Risto and hardly thought of him. I was teaching a new course and preparing the material took most of my time. Then one morning, I heard a knock on my office door and saw Sue Lannell's face. I flushed, then smiled self-consciously, wondering whether I should kiss her.

"Are you busy?" Sue asked. "I don't want to interrupt your work." She was wearing a blonde corduroy skirt and burgundy vest over a blue-button down shirt and looked like a graduate student.

"Who works?" I said, putting aside my papers and regaining some of my composure.

Sue sat next to the desk and looked at me and then away. She seemed serious but then she always seemed that way to me. It was what I liked about her. "I've come to talk about Risto," she said. "To ask a favor."

I nodded, encouraging her as I might an advisee, though I had no idea what she wanted. I had expected her to say something about us. "Anything," I said.

"I'm going to leave him, but that isn't really important, just inevitable. What worries me is that I'm afraid he's going to be fired. It would be hard to lose me and Kip, but I think losing his job would destroy him."

"Of course," I said, meaning to be conciliatory, but I could tell right away that I was in trouble.

"What do you mean, of course, Tony," she snapped. "Of course, as if it's nothing out of the ordinary. What the hell's the matter with you?"

"Sorry," I said. "I just meant, I understand."

"I don't think you understand at all. How could you, with your perfect little wife, your perfect little house and child and your nice little office? What problems do you have anyway? I can't think of any."

"Everyone has problems."

"Name one." And to my surprise all I could think of were trivialities: a five-pound weight gain; some minor surgery I'd had on my teeth; a lingering regret over my mother's death the year before; a suspicion that despite early promise I'd never do any really important work. Although I thought of myself as being involved in important projects, what it really came down to was a collection of little virtues, little vices. Then I felt angry. What right did Sue have to define the terms of my existence? Was a life without tragedy necessarily an unsatisfying one? Who could say what was small or large anyway? I knew I was mad at myself as much as Sue but that didn't matter. When had I started discounting myself, thinking of my problems as minor? I began to feel for the first time that I had a right to sadness, that sorrow might be the way out of the morass, and I needn't feel I served only as Risto's witness.

"What was the favor?" I asked.

Sue looked triumphant, then her expression softened. "I want you to talk to Risto's boss," she said.

"I had expected something more demanding, something that bore on our friendship. "What should I talk to him about?"

"Risto, of course. Maybe we can find a way for him to at least hold onto his job."

It was kind of touching that Sue was trying to protect Risto or soften his fall, even as she was leaving him. Risto seemed to serve that function for both of us.

"What do you want me to say? I've never even met Risto's boss."

Sue looked at me with a mixture of pity and contempt. "You're a man. You should know what to say."

I remembered Sue once talking about her father, about how he ran a dry goods business in Lexington, Kentucky, and survived the Depression because people were afraid not to give him credit. Now she wanted me to act like her father, to go to this stranger and talk some sense into him about Risto.

"Sue, I can't do that."

"You said you wanted to help, that you'd do anything."

"That's true"

"But when I ask a simple thing, not to lend us money or take him into your house, you refuse. I thought you were different, Tony, not like the rest of the people in this place. It's nothing to talk about sending money around the world to help starving children, what does that really cost you? But this would eat into your day, make your gym visit impossible, maybe embarrass you a little, and that's too much to ask. Forget it." She got up to leave, and I rose to stop her.

"Sue, I didn't mean that."

"What the hell did you mean then," she said, her eyes flashing with tears and anger. "It's fine to be the strong, responsible friend who picks Risto up when he's drunk. Fine to bring him home and even maybe bang the wife if she needs it, but..."

"Wait," I said. "Didn't you want that?"

"Sure, I did. I even think I deserved it. But didn't you want it too, Tony, even with your perfect little life?"

"Damned right," I said. "I want it right now" We stood there silently staring at each other, listening to the students walking by in the hall five feet away. Then the moment passed. In some way I knew that despite Sue's vitality it was really Risto I needed, his lack of responsibility, his ability to laugh when things were going to hell. He was my only contact with what I considered the illicit side of life. I didn't want to lose that. I sat down and picked up a pen. "What's the man's name?"

I was shown into Machen's office by a secretary in a red sheath. "Ten minutes," the man said to her as she left. He looked as I imagined Sue's father might have: tall, with a high forehead in a navy suit and suspenders. He wore his vest open with a red tie. "So" he began. "You're a friend of Lannell's." His eyes were sympathetic, friendly. "Lousy business. He's the best chemist I ever hired. Gave him a hundred dollar raise to come here from Chicago. I liked him too; still do."

I nodded. "His wife's afraid you're going to fire him."

Machen nodded. "She's a smart girl, business smart, not like Risto at all. He ought to be over at the U in one of those labs, less pressure there."

"So, she's right?"

"What can I do?" Machen said. "The guy's drinking cough syrup in the john on his breaks. Everyone notices and now the office girls are starting to laugh at him. I can't have that. This is a business, not a rest home."

Though he said nothing directly, because of his earlier mention of the University I had an idea where Machen thought the rest home was. "Can't you give him another chance?"

Machen smiled patronizingly, as if he was talking to a child. "He's had another chance, ten of them. Like I said, I like Risto, like him a lot. I've talked to him, talked to Sue, now I'm talking to you, and I don't even know who you are. I mean, I'm a reasonable man. We'd even send him to a program to dry out. But Risto doesn't listen. For a day or two he's all right, then his tests start turning out wrong because he gets sloppy. Yesterday, I returned from lunch and found him asleep on his desk. "I'm sorry," he said, rising to end the meeting. "Your buddy's out of chances."

HARD-HAT AREA

Charlie has called to say good morning to his daughter and finds himself discussing Hammurabi's Code. "How did they eat, dad?" Stacy asks.

Charlie is not ready for this. It's early and it's been a while since he's read much Babylonian law. "What?"

"The prisoners," Stacy asks. "After Hammurabi cut off their hands, how did they eat?"

Charlie imagines his daughter, all arms and legs with blonde hair in a ponytail. He has not spent one minute in his reasonably introspective life considering the dietary needs of Hammurabi's prisoners. He doesn't like being made to feel superficial by a seven-year-old, but the practicality of her question bothers him, too. Isn't Stacy concerned about the prisoners' suffering? Still, her question is the right one: No matter how awful the punishment meted out by life, survival is what really matters. "Maybe they had friends who fed them," Charlie suggests. "Or their families?"

"Like when I was a baby and you fed me?" Stacy asks.

"Yes," Charlie says. "Let me speak to mommy."

He waits a moment and then hears Becky's heavy sigh. "I've only got a minute," she says. "I've got to go to work."

"Are they discussing mutilation in the second grade now?" Charlie asks. "What is it, subtraction? If a man had two hands and they cut them off, how many would be left?"

"She started religious school last week," Becky says. "Is the Bible okay with you?" Charlie detects triumph in her voice. One of the concessions her lawyer negotiated was that he had to pay for Stacy's bat mitzvah.

"Isn't that upsetting for a kid Stacy's age?"

"I think it's fine," Becky says. "Got to go."

Charlie spends his day talking to clients. As a sideline to his regular job as a tax accountant, he has started a collection agency for psychiatrists. Charlie has never thought of himself as being particularly hard-nosed; he got the idea when a doctor he met at a party told him he was owed $87,000 and couldn't bear to ask his patients for it.

"I thought the fee was a part of the treatment," Charlie had said. "I thought it made people realize the doctor wasn't just a sympathetic friend."

The man nodded. "That's right, but I was a priest before I went to medical school, and I just find it very hard to talk about money."

Charlie collected half the money in a month, and the doctor was so pleased that he told his friends. Charlie is talking to one now, an attractive young woman two years out of medical school. "I'm not like Bruce," the woman is saying earnestly. "I really need the money."

The doctor has a nervous habit of smoothing her long brown hair over her ears as she talks. "You could refuse to treat them," Charlie says.

The woman looks shocked. "I can't do that," she says. "Don't you understand that these people are in pain?"

Charlie wonders idly if his creditors would accept that as an excuse, but he just smiles at the doctor. She probably does care about her patients, but she has a Mercedes, a house, kids in private schools, and a husband who is having trouble finding himself. All the doctors live that way, yet they act as if they exist under the most devastating privation imaginable.

"What if I contacted your patients?"

"You wouldn't say I told you to call?"

Charlie doesn't know how to answer. They are in a delicate area; money is always delicate. "Of course not," he says. "And if they complain, just tell them what philistines bill-collectors are."

He expects the doctor to smile at his joke, but she misses the irony. "That might work," she says slowly.

"Always works," Charlie says. "Count on it."

In the night, Charlie gets up because of a dull ache in his groin. His father died of prostate cancer, but everything seems okay. No blood, no pain. Except he's wide awake.

He sits at the table to eat a quarter of a watermelon. He lives in what is called a buffet in Denver--an efficiency anywhere else-- so everything is close at hand. Pinned by magnets to the refrigerator door are some of Stacy's drawings that seem unbearably poignant in the blue light. There is also a sign with a flowered border that reads, *"Hard-Hat Area."*

Stacy had seen the sign on a construction site one morning on a walk. Charlie remembers that it was a bad time in the marriage. He thought it might help if he took Stacy out for breakfast in the morning so Becky could sleep, but it didn't improve her mood. Something would always wake her and then they would fight out of frustration. Charlie knew Becky needed something he couldn't give her, but he wanted so badly to be the answer to her problems that he couldn't help being angry with her for needing something else.

Stacy started leaving signs around the house saying *"Hard-Hat Area"*, and Charlie knew it was because that was how life with her parents seemed to her. So Charlie left--not because he didn't love Becky and not because he was unwilling to work on the marriage. He didn't want Stacy to feel she was living in a danger zone. At the bottom, just above the zinnias, his daughter has written, "Love, Stacy," and this gives Charlie hope.

Charlie spends the day driving around the city. Denver isn't like New York. The freeways are inadequate to the demands of the newly arrived immigrants from the East, but no one seems to mind the traffic jams. Today, three Arabian stallions have gotten loose, and cars are backed up for miles while police officers leapfrog cars in pursuit of the horses. Charlie is on the horses' side. He imagines himself astride one of them, riding to freedom from the gridlock of life. The Arabians race around the cars, as if the freeway is nothing more than a giant show ring. The stalled drivers wait patiently as if they have nowhere to go. When the police finally corner them, Charlie feels disappointed and defeated.

Becky has left a message on his machine and for once her voice sounds warm. He had naively assumed that having known each other for twenty years, they would go on in much the same way after the divorce. It was the way other people talked about it, but for Becky the friendship ended with the marriage.

"You want life to be like a Woody Allen movie," she said one day. "Everyone wearing hats and thrift-shop dresses and saying funny-poignant things. Well, it's not like that for me, Charlie. It's not like that at all. You ruined my life, and I don't like you very much. I don't want to have lunch or talk about the things that matter to me because I don't trust you. Do you understand that?"

Charlie didn't, but he wasn't going to argue. "As long as we have Stacy we've got to try to get along," he said, wondering if he was using his daughter as an excuse.

"God, you sound like a self-help book," Becky said, and Charlie figured she was right. He'd been doing a lot of reading lately.

But now Becky is mysterious. "I need to talk to you," she says. "But not today. Maybe next week."

Her voice isn't cold, but it promises little, and this reminds Charlie of how things had been. They had always talked, endlessly, seamlessly. Then, somehow, that had stopped. Charlie blamed himself, but blaming didn't help. It was true that he had moved out, but Becky had left him first. When he reached for her in bed one night, she said, "Don't you have a secretary who needs a raise? I'm too tired." That was the end for Charlie, even if there was no secretary.

On the weekend he takes Stacy swimming, first splashing with her in the pool and then sitting in a chaise longue watching her brown arms thrash around. He wonders how something this perfect could come from such a flawed marriage.

For lunch, he makes hot dogs and macaroni and cheese, Stacy's favorite meal. "You're a great cook, dad," she says. "Mom never makes hot dogs. Could I have some orange juice?"

"I'm out," Charlie says. "How about a Coke?"

"OJ has vitamin C," Stacy says. "It fights nitrites."

Charlie looks at his daughter. "Nitrites?"

"In the hot dogs," Stacy says matter-of-factly. "Mom

read it in the paper."

"Think we could still get those nitrites tomorrow?"

"Oh, Daddy," Stacy says and laughs. "You're silly."

In that moment, he realizes she's right; he is silly and is happy to be. That's what he wants to give Stacy, his contribution: less Hammurabi and more silliness.

Charlie sleeps on the couch and wakes to Stacy's even, untroubled breathing. He had been dreaming, but now he can't remember the dream, only the suffused tone of sorrow that ran through it. When he was younger Charlie didn't regret many things. Not that he didn't make mistakes, but he didn't dwell on them; he considered occasional failure to be a necessary cost of living. Among the many things life has taught him is the need for regret.

In the morning, he makes pancakes. "Have you got any milk?" Stacy asks. "I need to cover the four food groups."

"Relax, it's in the pancakes."

Stacy looks thoughtful. "I guess that's okay," she says finally.

They play miniature golf at a place that has enchanted castles with moats at each hole. Afterward, Charlie buys Stacy ice cream and she doesn't mention the food groups or ask about any carcinogenic additives. When Charlie tucks her in bed, Stacy asks if she can have a wish.

"What do you want?"

"I want it to go on like this forever," Stacy says, and when Charlie gives her a questioning look, she adds, "I want you never to die."

Charlie tries to figure out what to say. Stacy's eyes are filling with tears. "Say you won't, Dad," she says.

The truth doesn't matter here, and Charlie doesn't care about the truth anyway. He holds his daughter close to him and whispers in her ear. "Okay, honey, I won't." Then again, fiercely now, "I won't."

Becky agrees to meet in a park near her office and Charlie gets there first, surprised by how anxious he is to see her. Finally, Becky arrives, out of breath and apologetic. "Sorry," she says. "We just hired a new girl."

One of Becky's conditions for having a child had been to quit her job, but being at home didn't agree with her. Charlie hasn't seen her in weeks, and she looks wonderful. What is most remarkable, though, is how happy she seems. It makes Charlie sad that this couldn't have happened when they were together. He'd still like to try again.

"Do you want to walk?" he asks. They always had, doing countless miles hand-in-hand while working through the problems of the day. That stopped when the baby came, but Charlie never resented Stacy for this. There is a cost for everything, and Stacy's price was the marriage. He'd pay it again.

"I'd rather sit," Becky says, but she smiles. She hesitates before continuing. Then she says, "I wanted you to know I've been seeing someone."

Charlie isn't exactly astonished, but it hits him. "That's good," he says cautiously.

Becky nods. "Actually, it's gotten kind of involved," she says quickly, looking to see if Charlie understands. Charlie doesn't know if he does or not. What's appropriate in this situation? Congratulations, a hug? He smiles weakly. "I didn't want to say anything before," Becky continues. She laughs again, nervous. "I mean, I didn't know if this would go anywhere, but now Reg and I... ."

"His name is Reg?"

"What's wrong with that?" Becky says, her voice rising.

Charlie has visions of country homes, cricket fields, or pitches. He has read somewhere that they are called pitches. "Is he English?" he asks.

"He's from Cleveland," Becky says. "He's different, Charlie. I can talk to him. He's really there for me."

Charlie knows Becky is only saying this because he asked about the name. They always talked about everything, and he was there for her, wherever "there" was. "Sorry," he says.

"It's okay," Becky says. "It is kind of a weird name." They both laugh. "Let's walk now," Becky says.

They start around the pond. Joggers and cyclists pass, and Charlie feels the urge to take Becky's hand.

"Reg would like us to live together," she says quietly.

"His place or yours?" Charlie asks, buying time. When he's hurt, he makes jokes; sometimes it works.

Becky isn't smiling now, very serious. "He has a big house; Stacy wouldn't have to change schools or anything."

"That's good," Charlie says. But his chest aches. To his embarrassment, he starts to cry--not sobbing, but leaking, water dripping onto his shirt. "Jesus," he says.

"I'm really sorry," Becky says, and he knows it's true, that she hadn't meant for this to happen either. In time the tightness lifts. "Are you okay?" Becky asks.

It is a stupid question, but Charlie nods. Okayness isn't really an option now, but he knows what she means. "You've got to go," he says. "Don't worry about me."

Becky looks doubtful, but she says, "I really should get back." She gives him a quick hug and leaves the park.

Almost on instinct, Charlie awakens in the night. He makes tea and goes outside. Things will move quickly now. Becky has managed the hard part, and he respects her for that. For some reason, Hammurabi comes to mind, and he imagines a sword falling with surgical precision. He would prefer that. If a man's hand offends, cut off his hand. Simple. Yet Charlie doesn't know how or whom he has offended or what his punishment should be.

It is warm but he feels chilled on the patio, waiting for sleep, waiting for light, perhaps just waiting for the waiting to be over. His night thoughts have become ritual for him, something he has forgotten to resist or resent. And yet he aches for something final, for this sorrow to end, and for his life to go on as he had always expected it would. As he sits along with tea in hand and dissection on his mind the foothills begin to glow in the distance. It is not much as portents go, but in his isolation, it makes Charlie unreasonably happy. He settles back in his chair to watch the dawn.

GUNSMOKE

Gunsmoke Harris was the first person I met when I reported for work at the old Pumping Station on Locust Street, and it wasn't a success. I hadn't planned to go on the job at eighteen, certainly not as a coal passer trainee and I wasn't happy about it. But I knew I was lucky to have anything at all, and wouldn't have if my uncle Billy hadn't had a friend in Public Works who owed him a favor.

Knowing this, however, did little to improve my mood. I had been in Madison trying to register for my freshman year when my mother called to say that my father had dropped dead in Riegleman's drug store. I knew the agony in her voice was due as much to having to call me home as it was to her loss, and this just made me mad at my father all over again. But there was no point in that anymore, and I knew without her saying anything that I would have to leave school and come back to Milwaukee. With three kids still at home, nobody had to tell me what my duty was, and my mother never would have anyway.

At the wake, everyone said this was only temporary, that I'd be back at the university before you knew it. Something would be worked out. I wasn't so sure. Our neighborhood was full of guys who had gone off once, returned home for some reason and never got away again. The East Side was like a sponge and having got clear once only to return, no one could tell me I'd be able to manage it again, short of a miracle. All I could think of was my family and teachers telling me at graduation I could make something better of myself--become a lawyer-- which might not have been much better after all. Now, all that was over almost before it had begun, and I was standing in the social hall at St. Pete's listening to my uncles bullshit each other about all the hearts they were breaking by staying married.

Which was all right and maybe all that I really deserved. but even if I wasn't going to be a big lawyer in a downtown office building, I had expected to end up somewhere better than the Pumping Station--maybe an apprenticeship at A.O. Smith or over at American Motors working on the line. But to get into the union you had to have someone stand up for you. Your father had to be a pipefitter before they'd let you inside. My old man got up every morning and went out like the others, but he never made it past Carey's where he drank his breakfast and spent the rest of the day dreaming of better things and writing poems, which he sang in a hoarse voice at weddings and funerals. Uncle Billy finally got him fixed up with something down at City Hall, but no one ever found out exactly what he was supposed to be doing and no in the family ever asked.

None of my friends looked surprised when I walked into Fran's that Friday night. Jack Baldwin just slid over in his booth and said, "We're going halves on a cheese and sausage. You want in?" and that was it.

Gunsmoke didn't care about my problems, though he knew I was from the neighborhood and had gone to East. He was small and taciturn and wore gray work clothes with pants that were sharply creased and broke just above his boots. Though we were indoors, he was wearing a gray cap with a cracked brim, and an unfiltered cigarette glowed between his thin lips. That morning, he looked me over with ill-concealed disgust and then turned away to spit. I was wearing a sport shirt and khakis. "First thing, better get you some work clothes." Then he tossed a long-handled broom in my direction. "Sweep the deck."

We were standing at the end of a long shop floor, and five or six men were watching with a mixture of curiosity and humor. Occasionally they'd call out, but Gunsmoke was all business. I took the broom and pushed it tentatively toward one of the huge blast furnaces. "No, goddamnit," he said. "That's it. You college boys think you know everything."

This wasn't really true, but I did think I knew whatever was necessary to sweep the floor. Gunsmoke took back the broom. "See that?" he pointed at the concrete floor.

A little blue cloud of ash had risen in the air. "No one could breathe in here if you swept the whole shop that way. Watch me."

He described a ten-foot area and began pulling the broom toward himself in short, brisk strokes. Though there was nothing artistic about Gunsmoke, there was grace in the long, flowing motion and in the ropey muscles of his arms. I also noticed that almost no dust stood in the air, despite the fact that a pile of soot three times as large as mine had accumulated.

It was hard not to admire the efficient motion, the ease with which the other man had done what I tried to do, even if on the face of it floor sweeping was of no particular importance to me. "Your way is better," I admitted.

"Damned straight," Gunsmoke said. Then he indicated the huge shop floor. "You've got some work to do, rookie."

It turned out that sweeping was a big part of my job and in time I was grateful for it. something about the languorous movement of the broom, and the fact that the task was never done--that there was always more ash--

comforted and enabled me to reconcile myself to my situation. With six blast furnaces working, soot was constant and everywhere. When I went out at the end of my shift, every car in the lot would be covered with a light shimmer of grime. Even at home, after showering, I would discover ashes beneath my nails or in my hair, and at the plant glowing cigarettes were everywhere, suggesting that if any of us were opened up somehow, we'd be smoldering inside too.

All of this, however, contrasted with the exterior of the Pumping Station, which had been built as a WPA project during the Depression and remained a point of pride for the mayor. Luxuriatnt lawns surrounded the building and in the vast public auditorium through which school children were herded at intervals, engineers in white coats tended to the gleaming turbines that dominated even that enormous room. Our crew remained safely hidden away in the back, and apparently few, if any, visitors ever wondered what powered the turbines, for I never saw a tour make its way to our foreman's desk, or peer into one of the furnaces. We were left alone, a small group of nondescript men in faded work clothes of whom little was known--or so it seemed.

Yet my job was not without danger and excitement. Three times each shift, I descended a metal staircase to the lower basement, a vast room under the furnaces with a low ceiling and a large fiery grate at one end. Wearing protective gloves and glasses, I would push a huge metal dolly beneath every furnace, center it under the door and then carefully wheel it open, watching always for flying cinders which according to legend, had put my predecessor's right eye out.

Despite the intense heat, however, I found the fire comforting, even alluring, and liked to feel the heat on my face. More than once, I leaned in close enough to singe my hair, and small bits of fire created a honeycomb in every shirt I owned. Yet I was not afraid. Indeed, sometimes I had to fight the urge to climb inside the gaping mouth of the furnace, for it was big enough, and often I imagined the fire being preferential to the reduced life I had outside. The banked embers were beautiful, mesmerizing, and I was transfixed by their heat. Then, appalled by my suicidal thoughts, I would pull back, sweating at my narrow escape.

After cleaning out the furnaces and depositing the ashes in the grate, I would go upstairs where the other men clustered around a battered desk in the middle of the floor playing cards and talking. I discovered there were barely two hours of work for each eight-hour shift and when, early on, I attempted to keep busy, the foreman growled, "Take it easy, kid. Save some work for the next shift."

I tried to keep up my education by reading during my breaks, but the idea of college inevitably faded as time went on. When registration for the new semester arrived, I let it go, rejecting even my mother's suggestion that I take a few classes at the extension. I was a worker now, a member of the city's union, and took pride in contributing to my family's support. My uncle co-signed a note for a Ford convertible, and I started going out with my old high school girlfriend, who was now enrolled in nursing school at Mount Mary.

Whether he had noticed these changes or simply because he had mellowed himself, Gunsmoke began to take a greater interest in me, though he still said little. He was an outsider in the group, a mystery man, about whom

I knew nothing, though I spent more time with him than with my mother or sisters. I didn't even know how he'd come by his nickname, though of course I knew about the television series and had even watched it irregularly when I was younger. Now I tried to remember, to re-enter that romantic world of the marshal and Doc and Miss Kitty, but my supervisor in his starched khakis and gloomy self-absorption seemed to have little to do with dance hall girls and gunfights. Still, I wondered as I noticed him watching me during the communal bull sessions that occurred each night after the front office closed and the bosses went home. Occasionally, a slight smile would crease his lips, but Gunsmoke never sat for long except when he'd been drinking, and then his eyes took on a bleak expression, and the old taciturnity would return.

Yet while Gunsmoke interested me, my curiosity was limited. Despite my new blue-collar identification, it was a difficult time in my life. I was rotating shifts and often got off work at two in the morning. By the time I had eaten and settled down it was four, and by seven the girls were up slamming doors, telling each other to be quiet. I had never had trouble sleeping before, but now the morning sun inevitably found its way through the blinds, and hearing my mother shushing my sisters as they got ready for school only made me feel guilty. Usually, I got up around nine. Then I would have breakfast and read in my room until it was time to go to work. Sometimes I would look at the bulletin board filled with notices celebrating forgotten dances and wondered whatever happened to that kid.

I was trying to hold onto the idea that I had options and was merely on extended sabbatical from my studies in Madison but reading Dreiser in the blue hours of the morning, I read myself onto the page and believed that what was coming was as inevitable for me as it was for the characters in the novel. Most of my friends were at work during the day, and to avoid thinking too much I started going to the plant early. There I'd sit in the locker room and play cards or roll dice with guys coming off the day shift until it was time to change clothes and go in myself.

In time, I came to feel comfortable there, sitting around the large circular tub where the men communally washed grime from their arms and creased foreheads, and complained about their wives. I had no wife and little to complain about, so I spent a lot of time listening, and my strangeness slowly faded until at last, I was accepted as one of them and my having been at college once was only a distant memory--one that seemed far less likely than the life I was living now.

During the long summer evenings, Dick, the foreman on the night shift, relaxed and allowed us to go outside where we lay on the wide lawns and traded cigarette coupons that would bring us impossible prizes in an unimaginable future. As long as the work got done, no one cared what else went on, and we all did our jobs faithfully. We washed our cars or fished in the river and once everyone brought food and a barbecue pit was constructed on the lawn. Guys wore Hawaiian shirts and danced the hula in a line before the banked furnaces. It was an all-male society, but I felt protected, even loved in that community; it seemed better to me than college could ever have been.

It was on one of these nights that I noticed a flurry at the plant door and saw Dick go over to talk to a woman I vaguely recognized. Their conversation was brief but intense as the woman shook her head back and forth and punched the air with her small fists. Then Dick was back at the desk, shoulders hunched as he dragged on an unfiltered cigarette. "Gunsmoke took off," he said simply, and I was suddenly ashamed that while I hadn't seen him for several days, I hadn't realized he was gone.

"Took off where? "someone asked.

Dick shrugged. "Gone," he said. "His old lady ain't seen him since Sunday. I been covering his ass here but sooner or later we've got to report it or its mine, aina?"

There was general assent to this. Everyone sympathized with Gunsmoke, though no one knew exactly why he had gone off. But Dick had a wife and three kids at home, and he had already taken a chance by not reporting Gunsmoke's absence. The rest of us could cover for a few days, especially since things were slow during the summer, but after that he would be on his own.

At first, the other men joked about it. It was suggested that Gunsmoke was just sleeping off a drunk and there was talk that he might be shacked up somewhere with a woman, though that seemed less likely. But after another day went by, Gunsmoke's absence began to cast a pall over the station. No one said anything directly, but what had happened opened the possibility that anyone could snap at any time without provocation.

Most of the men went straight home after work, but I was too keyed up to sleep and there was nowhere to go at that time of night. The sky was clear, and the moon hung over the river seeming to invite me. For reasons I didn't understand, I started walking south working my way downriver even if there wasn't much to see in the darkness. I'd gone about a half mile when I ran into Gunsmoke-- though at first, I didn't realize he'd been waiting for me.

He was seated on the flood wall with a glowing butt in his mouth looking at the river flowing by. "Hey," he said, as if we'd just happened to meet on the deserted river walk at three in the morning. He was holding a cane pole and every so often he would shake it but never pulled his line out of the water. I wondered if he was living off the river though it was hard to imagine what fish could survive in the dirty water. I didn't think he was really fishing. The pole was only his anchor.

"Hey, yourself," I said and stopped, unsure of myself.

"Take a load off your feet," Gunsmoke said and patted the cement as if it were an easy chair.

I sat down and we watched the river together silently. There was something soothing about it: the soft lapping of the water and the cars running over the viaduct high above us, their engines humming in the night. It was quiet and intimate. No one knew where we were, and this made it possible to say things that might otherwise be considered intrusive without being misunderstood. And I knew that Gunsmoke had invited this intimacy by hailing me.

"Your wife came by," I said, which at that time in that culture might have been interpreted as criticism. It would mean I knew he had deserted his family and left them without protection. But in the night, things were different: because it was dark, and we were alone. Gunsmoke knew I wasn't judging him for what he had done and was willing to help. I didn't ask why he had gone or where he had been for that would have been making the unwarranted assumption that I had a right to know. On the North Side, people often did violent and inexplicable things for their own reasons and were under no obligation to explain themselves. Gunsmoke would've been equally accepting if

Dick had reported him for not coming in. Yet I knew he was grateful to all of us for trying to cover for him.

"How is she?" Gunsmoke asked abruptly, which surprised me, for we had never talked about his wife. I didn't even know her name.

"I don't know," I said, which was true. I hadn't talked to her, had only seen her from a distance as she stood in the door gesticulating at Dick. "It looked like she was upset about something, though."

Gunsmoke nodded and I felt stupid. It was reasonable to assume that most women would be upset if their husbands were to leave suddenly with no explanation. But women and marriage were a mystery to me.

"I'm going to ask a favor," Gunsmoke said, surprising me again. But I felt honored by his gentle and courteous manner. In a similar situation, I might have shouted, made demands, expecting to be excused for it later. But Gunsmoke's soft, slow voice drew me in and made me like him in a way I hadn't before. "You don't want to do it, no harm done, no offense. But I'd like you to go to my wife and give her a message." Then he handed me a long gray envelope, like you'd buy at the A&P with the special lining so no one could hold it up to the light and read it.

I balanced the letter in my hand like a postal clerk. It seemed as if I should say something, respond in some way, but all the questions I could think of seemed inappropriate. I wanted to ask why he had chosen me, especially since it was clearly a choice. He had the letter prepared ahead of time and had followed me on my walk. I wanted to know where Gunsmoke had been staying for the last few days and how it felt to be away. I wanted to know how bad things had to get before you'd leave home and walk off the job.

It was the way I felt about my father, but you can't really blame someone for dying, even if I wanted to. I wanted to know if he needed money, food, or a place to stay. But there was no way to ask these questions, so I just said, "Sure," and put Gunsmoke's letter in my jacket pocket.

I didn't tell anyone at work what had happened because it would make no difference to Dick, and it wasn't anyone else's business. But the next morning, I put on my best pair of suntans and the only shirt I hadn't burned holes through and drove across the river to visit Gunsmoke's wife.

They lived in a duplex on the North Side and even though Gunsmoke had been gone a few days, you could tell the place was going downhill. There were boxes of paper on the dirty screen porch and a lawn mower had been left on the lawn to be stripped for parts by neighborhood kids.

I rang the bell, but it took a while for anyone to answer. When the door did open, I was facing a woman who was not much older than I was but had been beaten down by life. Her eyes were tired and dull and there were blue smudges on her cheekbones, as if she was bruised from the inside. She ran a hand through her brown hair and looked up at me. There was a momentary flicker of recognition as if she might know who I was and then nothing. She could tell I wasn't bringing good news and couldn't afford to give any of herself away. Two kids held onto her legs and a baby was crying somewhere in the back of the apartment. I was about to speak when I realized that I didn't know the woman's name. To call her Mrs. Harris seemed not so much formal as insulting, implying something about her age. Finally, I said, "Gunsmoke sent me."

While this didn't really explain anything, the woman stood away from the door and I followed her inside. "I'll make coffee," she said and walked down the hall.

I waited in the small living room which was oddly formal with damask-covered couches and flowered wallpaper. There was a cellophane runner down the middle of the white carpet, and I was careful to stay on it. The place was nicer than ours, which was furnished primarily by rummage sales and the Salvation Army. I wondered how Gunsmoke had managed to find the money, but was more curious about how he'd even have known such things as damask existed. It could be his wife, of course, but she hadn't struck me as that kind of woman.

Finally, she came in with a silver pot and cups and poured coffee. She looked less weary now and I wondered if my coming was a relief, if only because it broke the silence. I handed her the letter, but she didn't open it right away, turning it over in her hand meditatively, as if she wanted to prolong the moment.

"You said you saw Ralph?"

I was confused for a moment, but then I realized she meant Gunsmoke. I'd never heard anyone call him Ralph and felt the urge to smile. "Last night," I said. "After work, over by the river."

She thought this over for a moment and then nodded as if this made sense to her. When I thought about coming to her house, I had expected her to be angry—if not with me, then with Gunsmoke. I expected that because I thought she had a right. No one wants to be left, but a young woman with three children defined a special category. I wanted to help but even as young and inexperienced as I was, I knew I could do nothing. I could barely take care of myself.

Then she opened the envelope and read the letter. When she looked up, her eyes were glistening, but she didn't cry or tell me what Gunsmoke had written, and I didn't ask. She remained in her chair and I in mine and we drank coffee and acted as if this was a social call because it was important to her not to lose control. I was aware of the kids hovering in the hall, not letting their remaining parent out of their sight, but they didn't say anything either. I couldn't hear the baby anymore.

Finally, she put her cup down and spoke to me "You can tell him, it's okay," she said. I waited because I thought there would be more, but she was finished. I wanted to tell her I didn't know if I'd see her husband again and therefore didn't know if I could deliver the message. But her manner didn't encourage conversation. "I'll do that," I said, hoping I could find Gunsmoke and tell him what his wife had said.

Now she stood up, suddenly transformed in her flower-print housedress. Suffering had aged her, made her dignified rather than dowdy. "Thank you for bringing this over," she said. "We don't know you and you didn't have to do it, so thank you. It was kind of you to let me and the kids know about Ralph.

I felt she was exaggerating, that I hadn't really had a choice about delivering Gunsmoke's message, but I was being dismissed. I felt the urge to stay, to finish my coffee and talk more with this strange woman, but instead I set my cup down and left without asking Gunsmoke's wife what his letter had said and what was okay.

I never saw Gunsmoke again. A week went by, and Dick told management he was missing and reported it to the union. Three days later a new man named Gus with a rusty brush-cut and a ready laugh who was never at a loss for words showed up. I taught him how to sweep and push the coal through the furnaces but while we were together for another four months, I never felt anything for Gus, and I don't think anyone else did either. He was just there.

In the fall, my uncle turned up a half-scholarship for children of union men who had died, and my mother found a job in an office downtown. Those things and what I'd saved from the Pumping Station gave me enough to go back to college. In retrospect, it seems odd that I would have ever thought otherwise, but the guys gave me a sending-off party and told me my job would be there when I flunked out.

Even though most people would consider returning to the university an upgrade, I got on the bus to Madison with regret. I had come to think of myself as a man and valued the life and sense of maturity it had given me. While I had initially resented my inability to leave Milwaukee and my working-class destiny, I had found comfort and identity in the rituals of my job. What had changed me was not simply the work I had done but the idea of being a worker rather than some indistinct kind of professional. Now I was being stripped of that certainty. I understood coal and the men I worked with. I understood Gunsmoke and thought I understood why he had to leave. All of that was as clear as instinct, as natural as drawing a breath. But I didn't understand exactly why I was leaving now, only that I had to go, which was probably the way Gunsmoke had felt.

Among my regrets was breaking my promise to his wife, so a few days before I was to leave for Madison, I dropped by the duplex to see how she was doing, how the kids were. I rang the bell, but there was no answer. A pile of circulars and some unopened bills lay next to the door and the skeletal lawn mower still stood in the yard. I remembered sitting in the parlor that day, drinking coffee and Gunsmoke's wife trying to act as if things were under control. I asked the neighbors about them and where they might have gone, but there were only vague impressions. They seemed to have kept to themselves, avoiding others and whatever social occasions might occur on the block. No one knew anything specific about Gunsmoke or even his wife, though one woman did remember that a family with kids had lived in the house for a while. She didn't think they had a dog.

ARBORETUM

They say every tree in Denver has been planted due to our high desert climate. The green space adjacent to Greengate bears out this truth as only scrub grows there except for a few cottonwoods near the water, which is itself an artificial lake behind a dam constructed thirty years ago when the Army Corps of Engineers was in a down cycle and needed something to do.

Nevertheless, those who built our neighborhood in the Sixties dubbed this open space somewhat pretentiously as an "arboretum," a word that suggests a cultivated space crowded with exotic plants and trees, Japanese Elms, palm trees and the like. The area I'm speaking of, however, more nearly approximates a wasteland populated primarily by prairie dogs and snakes. Still, our arboretum is heavily used by residents and visitors alike. Runners jog there, others hike, walk their dogs, ride bikes and even camp across the woebegone lake in a dusty campground fronted by a small bathing beach. Teen-agers gather on the fringes during breaks from school and drink and smoke pot there at night. Perhaps as a consequence, more than one Greengate girl has lost her virginity in the arboretum, or so I've heard.

I'm no different than others in our community and was walking my dog Max in the arboretum one morning when I saw our friend Audrey sitting by herself hunched forward unnaturally on a bench, her forehead resting on her arms and knees. It suggested a Renoir, not a graceful pose, interesting but I saw quickly that aesthetics was far from Audrey's concern. She had been crying, her nose and eyes red, her hair askew, body tensed as if in fear of a punch. Anyone would have been affected by this and I was, but my response was more complicated because I could easily guess the reason for Audrey's distress. To make things worse, I felt responsible. I sat and put my arm around her shoulders while Max licked her hand. Far from comforting Audrey, however, this brought forth a new cascade of tears. She leaned against me and sobbed. "I want to die."

Disappointment in love is unlike any other disaster in life, and one for which there is no good remedy, not even new love. My feeling of responsibility, however, had nothing to do with personal involvement; I wasn't Audrey's lover and had no desire to be. Even when I was younger, I was no heartbreaker. In a sense, it was worse than that.

Like other friends of my wife, Audrey had teased me over the years, saying she'd like to clone me, claiming that most men were narcissistic assholes and not worth her time. Which made it seem odd that she constantly asked if I had any friends I could introduce to her. Most of my friends were married, happily or not, but in any case, engaged in long-term relationships and unavailable. This went on for years and then without warning one half of a couple we had previously imagined to be happy, disengaged himself and suddenly Joe Norman was single.

Joe had been a principal in a large technology firm before it collapsed during the recession that closed so many companies in Denver. Joe affected a lack of concern with this failure in our conversations and in fact celebrated his freedom from daily responsibilities by buying a Porsche and taking a vacation on St. Bart's. Now he was back in town, and he called to invite me to lunch. Although

I'd only known him before as half of a couple, it turned out we got along and our lunch evolved into a bi-weekly event at one of the few restaurants convenient to Greengate. When we got together Joe would inevitably pitch new investment opportunities that had come to him in mysterious ways through colleagues he never named. "That's great," my wife said when I mentioned this to her. "Take investment advice from a bankrupt loser."

This seemed a bit harsh, though I didn't really disagree. Joe told me he was now a consultant, but when I asked him what he was consulting about and to whom, his response defied understanding. My general feeling is that if someone can't say what he does in a few sentences, he's probably not being entirely honest. But Joe was still my friend. I assumed he was embarrassed about his situation and as a result obfuscation was his necessary companion.

I hadn't thought of Joe when Audrey asked about eligible men before, but he turned out to be a perfect candidate. He was tall, aristocratic-looking with thinning blond hair and faded blue eyes, belying what had actually been a blue-collar upbringing in the hardscrabble Vermont country south of Burlington. Audrey was short and Jewish, but she preferred gentile men, like her ex-husband, a charming pornographer straight from the social register who had been dismissed from Duke for cheating and was presently under indictment for mail fraud.

More than once, I had suggested that Audrey could learn from this mistake. What she really needed I said was a nice, retired jeweler whose wife had died, leaving him lonely and wealthy. But Audrey just rolled her eyes at this. "I'm not ready for a rest home," she said. She saw herself, not entirely unrealistically, as still being young, sassy and ready for fun. She said all the men she met online were losers, faked their pictures and were looking for someone to support them. Whether this was true or not is hard to say, but Audrey had high standards and as a result she had been alone for some years. Until Joe came along.

My wife and I often went to the movies with Audrey on Sunday afternoons and on one of these occasions, Joe happened to drop by, and we invited him to join us. Things developed quickly after that. Before long, we noticed Joe's car parked in front of Audrey's house on a nightly basis. The four of us would go out for dinner or just sit at home and watch movies. Joe and Audrey would sit close together holding hands and even my wife, the perennial cynic, admitted she'd never seen Audrey so happy.

"Maybe I should ask for a finder's fee," I said one day when the affair had been going strong for several months.

"Wait and see before you congratulate yourself too much," my wife said.

She was usually right, but day after day I'd wake up and go for the paper only to see Joe's Porsche parked haphazardly, one wheel up on the curb, in front of Audrey's house, as if he'd arrived in a hurry. Then apparently without warning, Joe disappeared abruptly, first supposedly on a lengthy business trip to London and then when he was supposed to have returned, not showing up for lunch and not answering phone messages or emails from Audrey. At first, she was just perplexed and a little annoyed. "He practically lives at my house for five months and then, poof, he's gone," she said one day, shaking her head as one might at a mischievous scamp.

But mysteries in life are seldom as perplexing as they first appear, and such was the case with Joe. Audrey turned out to be a guilty secret he kept from those closest to him. He hadn't introduced Audrey to his children or good friends except for us and this turned out to be a portent of things to come. To make things worse, he had had a habit of calling escort services when he needed a date, something I knew but had decided not to share with Audrey. I had no personal knowledge of the shadow world of hired sex, but I wasn't naïve and didn't even disapprove. I knew escorts existed for the pleasure of businessmen like Joe and figured they served a need. Still, I had assumed all this was in the past and that it would be up to Audrey to change Joe's wandering ways. Joe's sexual history wasn't my problem.

Now, however, I felt I should have been more careful. Whether I wanted to think so or not, I was as involved in Audrey's affair as any *shadchan* in a Ukrainian village. I should have been more careful in my recommendations or, better, left well enough alone. Which is why I was sitting on the hot bench with Audrey this morning in the Arboretum.

After a time, Audrey stopped sobbing and seemed more quiescent. "What really pisses me off is I should have known. After being married to Fred, I should have seen the signs."

"What signs?" I asked.

"That he was a sociopath."

Fred was her ex-husband. I didn't really feel like defending Joe but comparing him to a person who had a federal court date seemed extreme. "Sociopath?" I said. "Has he broken the law?"

"Who knows but you don't have to to be a sociopath," Audrey said, with the assurance she showed on all matters.

"He understands the difference between right and wrong; he just doesn't care. That's enough. I've been talking to his ex-wife. Turns out we have a lot in common."

Choosing another woman over Audrey didn't seem to rise to level of sociopathy, but I knew his ex-wife would not speak kindly of Joe. "You've met Liz?"

"I made it my business to meet her," Audrey said. "Did you know Joe Norman had been married before?

"Before Liz?" This was news to me.

"At least once," Audrey said darkly. "And who knows how many other times."

Joe was taking on epic stature among local villains, and I had a sneaking admiration at his having been able to hide this behind the hedges and shrubs of a suburban lifestyle for years. "I didn't know" I said.

"But you knew about the escorts, right?"

"I did," I admitted. "I should have told you."

"Damned right," Audrey said, then she patted my hand to let me know she didn't hold it against me. "It's okay. He had everybody fooled."

"I'm really sorry," I said.

"It's not your fault," Audrey said.

"I feel like it is."

"That's because you're a nice guy," Audrey said. "You don't understand evil."

"I suppose not," I said, but this didn't change anything. I thought of myself essentially as being an outsider, uninvolved even as I watched with interest the goings-on of my neighbors. But I knew at base I was kidding myself, even before Audrey got dumped by my friend. Listening, watching, *was* involvement as truly as what Joe had done. It was just more subtle.

Time went by but whenever we saw Audrey Joe's name came up, usually in connection with a serial killer or some nut who'd shot up a school. It would not only have done no good to point out the difference. "Maybe it's what she needs to do to get over it," I suggested to my wife one night.

"If so, it's not working," she said. "She's just as hurt and angry as she was a few months ago."

"She's not obliged to get over it," I said. "Maybe we just want her to."

My wife nodded. "Sure, except it's no way to live, angry all the time."

"It's her anger," I said. Sometimes it helped to state the obvious, but the fact was I wanted to do something, not just for Audrey's sake but my own.

I checked the internet, but Joe wasn't involved in any lawsuits and there were no judgments against him. Broken hearts didn't count. He wasn't on Facebook, Linked In, or a dozen other sites, and when I checked his phone number had been changed. I started to wonder if he'd been a phantom and never really existed in the first place, though I knew he had. We'd known him long before he started dating Audrey. He had just disappeared.

"Let it go," my wife said. "Why persevere? You're not a P.I. Maybe you have too much time on your hands."

This stung as it resonated with other comments she'd made over the years about my working at home. I knew it wouldn't bother me if there wasn't truth to what she said, but it didn't make it easier. Once, frustrated by the implications of my laziness, I had bought a time clock at Office Depot and clocked in each morning. This had a good effect as my wife apologized and admitted she was jealous of my free time and ability to organize my life. Still, it remained a dormant issue. "I'm just curious," I said now.

She looked skeptical. "Sure," she said. "Actually, you're more like a dog with a bone. What would you do if you found something incriminating anyway?"

"Maybe I'd feel vindicated," I said. "Like he was a con man who'd fooled lots of other people and there was a reason I was stupid enough to fix him up with Audrey."

"Do you have any idea how crazy that sounds?"

Being called crazy by a specialist will make you stop and think but the truth was I had no idea what I was looking for or why, only that it seemed important to persevere. Generally, I don't question my instincts even if more than once they've led in disastrous directions. I continued to surf the internet and search my memory for clues. Then one afternoon when I'd started to think Joe was really a chimera, I saw him sitting in the Tuxedo Lounge nursing a beer. The Tux was the only bar convenient to Greengate, and it seemed to be Joe's way of announcing his re-entry into our world. He looked exactly as I'd always thought of him, at ease, long legs wrapped around a bar stool, raising his right hand in emphasis in what appeared to be mid-argument with the bartender.

Rather than approach him immediately, however, I decided to sit in my car and observe. Why? Instinct again, but I'd become a stalker with no clear purpose. Perhaps I wanted to strategize, to think over what I'd say to him when we talked but the fact is my mind wasn't clear on the subject. I just didn't feel like going inside yet. I hunched down in the seat and thought about movies I'd seen about stakeouts. I remembered cops drinking stale coffee, eating fast food, pissing into cups while they waited for their prey to make a move. I had only an empty Starbucks cup, but I figured that it would serve the purpose if necessary and settled down to what I expected to be a long wait. In stakeouts, I knew you were supposed to move your car every few hours so the person you were watching didn't "make" you, but there were no directions on what to do if you had to get home for dinner. I decided to give it an hour or so and see what happened.

An hour passed, Joe remained in the bar, and I began to feel stupid sitting in the car watching him. Finally, still with no clear plan in mind, I got out and went inside. When Joe recognized me, he signaled with a lazy wave as if his arm were made of macaroni. It was as if we'd seen each other yesterday. I wasn't sure how to respond to this but at this point escape was impossible. I seldom patronized the Tux in mid-afternoon or even truth be told, at night but there we were. I sat next to him and ordered a beer. "It's been a while," I said.

Joe nodded. "I've been busy lately."

He didn't say what he'd been busy doing and I knew enough about his circuitous answers not to ask. There was no telling what Joe had actually been up to and I doubted he would say. "Audrey missed you," I said, jumping into it.

Joe looked at me with interest, his eyes narrowing. "Is that right?" he asked.

"Of course," I said. "For months you're there all the time and then suddenly without warning you're gone."

He smiled. "I wonder if most people announce they're leaving in situations like that," he said thoughtfully. Then "Sounds like you have a personal interest in this."

"I do," I said. "She's my friend. I'm the one who introduced you in the first place." Joe's languid pose was beginning to irritate me beyond anything rational.

"So, you feel responsible in some way?"

He sounded like a counselor or social worker, and I resented his condescension even as I believed I'd earned it. "Damned right," I said. "I should have known better."

He nodded. "Oh, I get it," Joe said. "You should have known somehow that if you introduced us, we'd like each other initially but in time we'd decide the relationship couldn't last?"

"Is that what you think happened? That the two of you decided together? Audrey seems to think you just walked away without saying anything."

Joe shrugged. "Say that's true. Don't I have a right to do it? Is there some rule that I have to endure hours of psychobabble about how immature I am, how unable I am to face up to responsibility and God knows what all?"

I hadn't thought of it this way. What Joe was talking about was exactly what I would have expected to happen if I were in a similar situation. But I wasn't and he was, and this was how he'd decided to handle it. Did that make him a sociopath, as Audrey said? The only thing to do at this point was to drink some beer so that's what I did.

"So that's all there was to it, the disappearing act?" I said, thinking I had him.

Joe spread his hands wide. "Like I said, I was busy. But here I am and here you are and we're talking so what difference does it make how long it took or what I did? Anyway, I wrote you an email a while back and you didn't answer. Since we're being frank, what was that about?"

He was right. He'd cut Audrey and I'd thought I would cut him. This was all turning around on me, and I no longer felt in possession of the truth about what had gone on. "I didn't think we were still friends," I said lamely.

Joe smiled thinly. "We were friends before I ever met Audrey, and we were friends while I was seeing her, but now all of a sudden, it's a requirement of friendship for me to treat her some way you think is fair? Who made you judge and jury of all this?"

The way he put it made me sound unreasonable, but I held onto the notion that I had behaved honorably, and he hadn't. "No, not judge and jury, but just knowing what's right or something like that. It's not really that hard."

"Interesting," Joe said, but we both knew it wasn't. I'd lost the high ground, and Joe was fencing with me.

I thought of Audrey branding him a sociopath and tried a new tack. "Let me just ask you," I said. "Do you understand that the way you treated her was wrong or is it that you just don't give a shit one way or the other?"

Joe smiled lazily. He was enjoying this much more than seemed appropriate. "I'm still stuck on the idea that it's any of your business," he said. "You introduced me to your neighbor, we were together for a while and enjoyed each other, or at least I did. Then at some point it got old, and it didn't make sense to go on anymore."

"For you."

"Of course, for me. Who else are we talking about? Who else could I possibly speak for."

"Audrey maybe?"

Joe shrugged theatrically. "Maybe if I could read minds or if her life was my responsibility. If it seemed over to me, I figured it was the same for her or would be before long."

"Did you ask her?"

Joe laughed. "Are you serious? What are we, in junior high? You're saying I should ask the woman I'm seeing if she's as tired of me as I am of her. Who does that?"

I stood there stupidly, astonished that anyone could apparently care so little for the feelings of someone he'd been intimate with. "Does it matter to you at all that she's miserable over this, has no idea why you did what you did to her?"

"Too bad," Joe said. "But to be clear, I didn't do anything to her."

"She's doing this to herself?"

"Beats me," Joe said. "I don't understand why women think the things they do. It's always been a mystery to me. Part of what's so fascinating about them, you know?"

"Fascinating," I repeated.

"Completely," Joe said, and our conversation was over.

My meeting with Joe left me feeling dissatisfied, not just with his smooth evasiveness, but with myself. Though I enjoyed thinking of myself as being a mere observer of the foibles and foolishness of my neighbors, there was no denying that I'd become involved in Audrey's unhappy love affair. Despite her willingness to absolve me, I couldn't absolve myself. I had gone into the Tux determined to confront Joe for his insensitivity and make him take responsibility for Audrey's despair and I had failed miserably. Joe had pointed out that his behavior was no business of mine and now I realized that much as I might dislike what had happened, he was right.

Finding someone for Audrey after her years alone had appealed to me but why? Was it my way of vicariously experiencing a love affair I'd never enter into myself? There was something undeniably titillating about looking across the street at Joe's car parked in front of Audrey's house and thinking of them locked in a passionate embrace, but I wasn't really interested in Audrey sex life. So, what was it then? Had I expected something like credit for arranging the perfect match, something more than simple thanks? This was closer to what I might reasonably expect, though what this might be I couldn't imagine. It would be nice to think you'd affected someone else's life positively, solved a previously insoluble problem but that elevated Audrey's loneliness to unrealistic standards.

The fact was I didn't know why I'd really become involved, but I knew I'd been grandiose in my confrontation with Joe. I could neither take credit for mutual attraction between two people nor assign responsibility to one or the other if things didn't work out tempting as that might be. Audrey would have to be miserable as long as this was necessary for her, and her friends would have to tolerate it. My wife as always saw things in a less complicated way.

When I described my meeting with Joe at the Tux with my wife, she lay the dish towel on the sink and said, "I always thought he was nice," she said. "For a guy."

"What does that mean? What else could he be?"

She shrugged. "Just that Audrey expected too much. After all, he'd been divorced twice, that tells you something."

"So, he shouldn't have behaved better, couldn't have helped dumping her the way he did?"

She smiled. "Look at Sir Galahad. No, that's a little deterministic for me. Sure, he could have stayed around but you can't necessarily expect him to just because that's what you think you would have done if you were in that situation. No one's really required to do the right thing.

She got five months out of him, which is more than anyone else in recent memory. Maybe Audrey's just tough on people. Ever think of that? In fact, I'd bet that part of what she liked about him was that he wasn't a nice guy, just like her ex-husband."

She had me. I hadn't thought of Audrey's part in her own misery because I was focused on what I thought of as my responsibility for the breakup. "It's not my fault for introducing them?"

Now my wife surprised me. Dropping her ironic tone, she leaned over and kissed my cheek. "Such a sensitive guy," she said. She cradled my neck for another minute. Then she said, "Look, it was nice of you to introduce Audrey to Joe, nice for both of them, at least for a while. Maybe a little too nice, to be honest. But that's the end of it. Audrey's not blaming you; why blame yourself?"

The trouble with inarguable logic is that you can't really dispute it. I still felt foolish about my encounter with Joe and guilty for having set him up with Audrey, but I now saw it was my own fault in both cases. There was nothing to do but go on as I had, even if, as I suspected, I'd really learned nothing. The next morning Max and I were out early in the Arboretum as usual. Since it was early we were alone except for snakes and the occasional coyote. We made the circuit once and then on the way back I saw Audrey sitting on the bench, though now she was dry-eyed, which I guessed was an improvement. I debated telling her I'd seen Joe but decided against it, so perhaps I had learned something.

I took the seat next to her and put my arm around her shoulders. "Nice day," I said, indicating the blue sky.

"Sure," she said. "For now."

"Well, there's no guarantee it will last, I guess."

"Exactly," Audrey said.

We both laughed and while I didn't ask, I assumed she was feeling better. She was right. There were no guarantees. She was entitled to a relapse or whatever a resurgence of tragic resonance in these matters might be called. Joe might even re-emerge at some point, though I doubted this would happen. It was all part of life's grand pattern, or at least that part of it that was revealed to me.

ERUV

It started small, two rooms in an office building adjacent to a strip mall with a Safeway and a branch bank. One day a sign appeared on the door: Jewish Enlightenment Center, Rabbi Yakov Blitz, Leader. No one knew what to think about that, though Dotty Adams remarked that she hadn't known there were any Jews in the neighborhood and some patients of the optometrist next door were made uncomfortable by the men's long black coats and broad brimmed hats. They wondered if the men were Goths, like those boys at Columbine. But someone pointed out that those boys weren't Jewish which put a stop to that.

Within three months another office became available when an actuary with a small suite relocated to Cherry Hills Farms and then within a year the whole third floor was occupied by the Jewish organization. Activities increased accordingly. Now, in addition to Shabbat services on Saturday, there were gatherings for religious dancing and even a boys' klezmer band that people as far away as the liquor store could hear tuning up on weekends. Yet while men in traditional black clothing, women in bowl-shaped wigs, and little boys with paes and tzit tzit hanging beneath their sweaters now frequented the kosher section in the grocery store, no one complained. Some people thought the Jews might be actors.

In fact, no one in our neighborhood said a word until Blitz and his followers purchased the New Zion church on the corner after the Lutherans moved out. First it was Koreans in the old Baptist church and now a Jewish community down near the corner. Someone said the neighborhood was beginning to look more like Brooklyn than a suburb in Colorado. The person who said this had never been east of Limon, but the point had been made. Things were changing and most people felt change was seldom for the better.

Still, the gatherings at the new synagogue remained largely peripheral to our lives. There had always been a few Jewish families in our neighborhood, of course, but they were quiet and seemed much like everyone else, the women in mini vans, the kids in ripped jeans, the men going off to work in the morning as lawyers, doctors, or accountants. People reassured themselves about their open-mindedness, their lack of prejudice. Everyone got together at the neighborhood parties, though some of the Jews seemed uncomfortable at Oktoberfest when Charlie Schmitz wore lederhosen, played Wagner on his huge speakers and sang loudly until he got too drunk to stand up. And despite the vague uneasiness at the new presence of strange strangers, things were much the same in the neighborhood. Sandy Irvine, who lived next door, sank deeper into the mystery of Alzheimer's. Ed Williams toured the neighborhood with his earphones and sunglasses shielding him from the world. Grass was mowed, children were taken to lessons, small tragedies and triumphs occurred as they always had, in private and away from the notice of others.

Everything changed when the eruv was created. The first we heard of it was when we saw men in long hair and hats up on ladders running what looked like a guy wire around the village south of ours and then ours, extending east to the state park line and south four or five blocks to Havana. Some assumed they were from the phone company or maybe fixing the cable which seemed to go out whenever there was a high wind. But in time a circular arrived on our porches announcing that Yakov Blitz had created a "symbolic religious enclosure in which pious Jewish residents could carry on their daily activities on the Sabbath." Beneath this was the crest of the village government so apparently the whole thing was legal. There were mutterings that the Jews had bought off the town commissioners but still there were no serious complaints because no one knew what this eruv really was.

Chuck Shapiro, who pronounced his name ShaPIEro, had once lived in Omaha and claimed to be familiar with this sort of thing. Chuck explained that really religious Jews weren't allowed to work outside their homes on the sabbath. Even tasks as small as carrying a box were considered work so the establishment of an eruv allowed them to consider the whole neighborhood to be their homes. This seemed like playing fast and loose with God's law, but Chuck told us that was normal for Jews, that they carried on like this all the time--and finagling was almost an art form with them. It was clear this caused Chuck a certain amount of embarrassment, though it did make him feel more important than he had since he was a judge at the village ice carving contest.

"I don't know," Dottie Adams said. "It don't seem all that normal to me."

Dottie wasn't much of a moral relativist, but her meaning was clear. The newcomers weren't like the people in our neighborhood, many of whom had been among the first to settle this area thirty-five years ago, often coming from as far away as Kansas and Missouri. They were drawn by clean air, open land and good schools and many had stayed on even after their children had grown up and gone away. Now we had mature vegetation and while the city had grown up around us, the state park was still adjacent to our community which until now had made us feel insulated from change. Neighbors came and went in the complex rhythms of life, you accepted that. But this was different. This felt like an invasion, like Joseph taking his people down into Egypt. You read the Bible and Joseph's a hero, but how did the Egyptians feel about that little excursion?

What seemed odd about this was that while you'd expect an eruv to have natural boundaries like mountains or a river, this one had just been dropped in the middle of sixty-five quarter acre homes on the Colorado prairie. Why here, was the question? We all liked our neighborhood, but it didn't seem especially Biblical. Why hadn't Yakov Blitz taken his flock into North Denver where most of the Jews in town lived, or since they had gotten money, into Cherry Creek? Why a small suburban community that had, at most, four Jewish families living there?

Before anyone could answer this question, however, another circular arrived, this one announcing a meeting of the zoning committee to consider an application for expansion of the new synagogue, in order to provide space for a Hebrew school and summer camp. Rabbi Blitz' flock had grown and the Lutheran church was no longer equal to the congregation's needs.

Before this meeting could be held, however, more mail arrived, this being a letter from a lawyer in Boulder offering to buy our houses "above market, no broker involved." The attorney claimed he represented a friend who wanted to live in the area. And while it seemed a bit intrusive, Dottie Adams was enjoying the attention. "I never used to get mail," Dottie said. "Just those damned emails from my kids. Now I get a real letter every day and they all have Hebrew writing. I feel like I'm living in Israel or something."

Others were less pleased by the solicitations, though, especially when we discovered that Art Sellers had sold his house with the help of the Boulder lawyer whose client turned out to be a follower of Rabbi Blitz. Then the Crawfords over on Elmira sold and before you knew it there were five new families, all with kids wearing skull caps as they rode their bikes around the neighborhood.

"I don't care if they're Jews or Moslems or what they are," Earl Daggett said, "but they could at least say hi when you see them on the street. It's like some kind of goddamned cult or something."

It had always been the protocol in our neighborhood to wave as cars went by, to greet one another as we walked our dogs, to attend the neighborhood parties, small and superficial rituals but important to everyone. Yet the new arrivals attended nothing, greeted no one and kept to themselves, except on Shabbat when we'd see them walking *en masse* toward the synagogue black coats swaying in the summer breeze, women deep in conversation, kids running around their parents and somehow avoiding the traffic. After services they'd troop back to one house or another, often bringing friends with them for dinner, which would last long into the night with much laughter and hilarity for all to hear.

It might seem reasonable to wonder if part of the neighborhood reaction had to do with envy for people who seemed whole in themselves, found what they needed in obscure customs and cared little for general approval. People who didn't seem to care what their lawns looked like, what cars they drove, or how they dressed even if they had the money to buy our houses, fund a new wing on their building and buy their rabbi a late model Mercedes. But if people were resentful no one admitted it. Despite some dark mutterings about rich Jews buying their way into the neighborhood and the comments about social snubs, if things had gone no further than this people would have adjusted, just as they did when the Pope brought thousands of people in for a mass at the state park in '92 and the kids trampled everyone's lawns and smoked pot down by the lake.

Soon, however, an electric sign appeared on wheels in front of the synagogue announcing new initiatives of Rabbi Blitz. It wasn't enough to keep the activities of the synagogue within its walls; now the rabbi was reaching out to Jews driving by on Belleview Avenue or anyone else. In addition to the Hebrew lessons, there was an adult study group that met regularly. "Lessons of the Shulchan Aruch, Halacha and Modern Life," the sign proclaimed one week and "Mysteries of the Zohar Revealed" the next. Then it was "Pentateuch and You, Listening to Torah."

It was as if a new theatre had opened specializing in cabbalistic subjects. While there had long been a study group in the neighborhood and every year children walked around with charcoal smears on their foreheads during lent, these practices weren't seen as revolutionary or disturbing in the same way as Yakov Blitz' latest initiatives.

Whether it was the sign or something else, however, new people were appearing daily on the streets of our neighborhood. There was an article in the paper about the synagogue and its leader with Yakov Blitz pictured in a black suit and big-brimmed hat wearing a quizzical expression on his face. And while we had heard that traditionally Jews were opposed to missionary work, the article said Blitz was drawing his congregation from as far away as Longmont and Fort Collins. Who even knew there were Jews in those towns? The article went on to say that disaffected members of other congregations like the Jewish Educational Alliance over in West Denver and Congregation Emanuel in Hilltop had broken from a more liberal path to follow a new, more exacting spiritual leader.

What's more, Blitz turned out to be good for business. Since the pious couldn't drive on the Sabbath, followers who hadn't yet bought houses in the eruv, drove to our neighborhood and booked rooms on Friday night at the Marriott or the Hyatt. Since weekends were dead times for the hoteliers, they began to offer what they called Shabat Sales, where the faithful could get a room and a kosher meal blessed by the rabbi for less than it would cost to book during the week.

On Saturday morning, you could see a pious army in satin wrappers and beaver hats, issuing from hotel row up the hill to the synagogue and then back after Havdalah, which marked the end of the Sabbath. No one was sure what went on in the little building during the rest of the day but soon there were basketball nets and a volleyball court on the side for the kids and while the new congregation did nothing that could be considered disruptive, there was no question that Blitz and his followers were here and growing by the day.

An enterprising Korean dry-cleaner advertised special rates for the kaftans and fedoras and promised faithfully to have them "Ready for Shabbos." There was talk of a kosher deli opening in the strip mall where the rabbi had been located and someone said he'd heard Blitz now had a real estate interest in the shopping center and was negotiating with a kosher butcher for space when the Radio Shack lease was up. People weren't sure they wanted to live in the upscale Jewish ghetto that was developing, but there wasn't much choice, unless you decided to move and perhaps as a result the rate of sales escalated through the summer. It was a Yiddish version of blockbusting, in which greedy realtors scared gentile home-owners with stories about declining property values if more Jews moved in.

Of course it was actually the opposite, a sort of real estate gold rush with people getting prices they had never dreamed. Jim and Anne Simmons, who had been among the first to move to the neighborhood and had purchased their house for sixty-five thousand thirty years ago, closed with a young couple from Baltimore for ten times that. And now wealthy parishioners were buying houses to use only on Fridays, which insulted some of the neighbors more.

"They're making us look bad," Bob Schultz said one night. "I mean, we have to live here all the time. With the money they've got they can buy a house for one night a week and maybe the High Holy Days."

It was impressive that Bob knew what to call the period between Rosh Hashanah and Yom Kippur, but he didn't apparently think of comparing buying a house for religious purposes with the cabin he owned in Silverthorne where he went skiing a few weeks a year. Irony dogged us, but as time went on resentment toward the Jews grew.

Not everyone reacted with either anger or dismay, however. One morning I saw Sandy at her customary post by the mailbox and went down to talk to her, as I usually did to make sure she was all right. Sandy looked at me with a direct, unblinking stare. She had no idea who I was though I'd lived next door for ten years. "I'm in a movie," she said, more to herself than to me.

I tried to imagine this as she might have. Her life was going by, and she was only watching, not participating, or she could have been saying simply that it all seemed unreal, life, death, what lay in between. It was a more thoughtful comment than most of my neighbors would make, and it was odd because Sandy was the only one losing her mind. I asked what she meant.

"Fiddler on the Roof," she said. Then she turned and went back indoors. It made more sense than most of what I'd heard for the last month or so.

Some people seemed curious if not exactly interested in the interlopers and a few started trying out various terms they'd heard on late night TV. Walking my dog Max, I stopped to chat with Ed Williams who always has time on his hands. For once he had taken the earphones off so I asked how he was. Ed threw his arms wide and said, "Tsuris, that's how. You got kids, you got tsuris, that's all I know." He bent down and patted Max on the head. "You know what I mean, don't you, Max." Max was childless, but he always looked sympathetic which seemed to be enough for Ed who now shook his head and went back into his house.

Tension grew as the date approached for the meeting with the zoning board. By now there were eight families in our part of the eruv and as if to mark the precipitous growth of that community, some kids dislodged the wire marking the eruv in the middle of the night and threw red paint at the east wall of the synagogue. Someone also hung toilet paper from the cottonwoods in front of one of the houses and in the morning, it hung down in pristine white tendrils over the lawn.

TPing a house was generally reserved for those residents who had pretty young daughters and some felt this could have simply been a mistake, but no one offered to help clean up. It hardly mattered. Used to discrimination, pogroms and worse, twenty Jews were out the next morning on ladders, removing the toilet paper and replacing the wire marking their domain. In their black pants and yarmulkes, they reminded me of so many crows on a telephone line, bending to their work, ignoring the world around them.

If members of Blitz' congregation were upset or blamed anyone besides restive teenagers for their inconvenience, it didn't show in their attitude toward us. They remained as distant as ever but not more so. Perhaps as a comment on all this, the message on the sign in front of the synagogue this week read: "Make Misvoth Matter." But beyond the alliteration it was unlikely this advice had much effect since no one who lived in our neighborhood was likely to know what a mitzvah was.

Because of the attention the re-zoning petition had received, the board decided to meet in the auditorium of the Middle School rather than at City Hall as usual. It was hard to know how large Blitz' congregation was, nor who might be residents of our village and who merely interested onlookers, but the Jews arrived early and settled in the front of the room, all dressed in black as usual, men and women separated by an aisle as if preparing for worship. To the right were three young women with notebooks who seemed to be representatives of the press. Bored camera men in jeans and sweatshirts with television cameras on their shoulders leaned against the wall waiting for something newsworthy to happen. The rest of us filed in and sat here and there, perhaps a bit embarrassed both by our new interest in zoning matters and the recent acts of harassment toward the Jews.

The chairman of the board was a man named Hal Congden who'd lived in our neighborhood for years and was an expert on the village bylaws. This had come out a year ago when he objected to asbestos tiles being put down on someone's roof, pointing out a little-known sub-section of the village code that it turned out he'd written on a slow day in 1987. Hal hadn't ingratiated himself with the homeowner in question that day but everyone was impressed with his knowledge of the law and willingness to enforce it, which accounted for his position on the zoning board.

Tonight, perhaps impressed by the gravity of the occasion, Hal was wearing a tan blazer, blue shirt and striped tie, though it was a warm night and the air conditioning in the school wasn't really keeping up with the crowd. After letting people get settled, he tapped his gavel on the table in front of him and said, "Okay, nice to see everyone tonight." Then he looked to his left and asked to have the minutes of the last meeting read aloud. The secretary was a middle-aged redhead who looked tired and nervous. She read in a halting singsong and seemed incredibly relieved when she had finished. Hal asked for additions or corrections and seeing none called for new business.

At this Yakov Blitz himself rose and addressed Hal. "Mr. Chairman, there is the matter of our request to enlarge our place of worship." He pointed to the table. "There, it's in front of you, I believe."

Most of us had never heard Blitz speak and may have expected him to have a heavy Yiddish accent. Instead, his voice was polished, oracular, his words resonating in the room decorated in blue streamers exhorting the Mustangs to victory. Blitz was a small man with a big voice and dapper in a blue suit, impressive in an area given to informality. You wouldn't have said he was handsome with his small stature, forehead laddered with wrinkles and thinning hair, but he had force, which shouldn't have been surprising given the success he'd had building his congregation in a short time. What was more unusual was his obvious sincerity and even modesty. There was neither swagger nor Swaggert about him and now we bent forward involuntarily to hear.

"Where's that dude from?" Ed asked in a stage whisper. "I never heard a Jew talk like that before."

Ed's knowledge of Jews and Judaism was limited, as was true of the rest of us, but the question was legitimate. Blitz seemed to have descended from somewhere unknown, a man with no background we knew of, apparently unmarried and without attachments, a rabbi in a strip mall but one clearly on the move. Now Hal cleared his throat. He looked at the pile of papers in front of him and squinted through his tri-focals at them. "Well, now, Mr. Blatz," he said, amidst some snickers. "It seems like what you want to do is make your church bigger, is that right?"

Blitz smiled thinly, too savvy to be bothered by Hal's mangling of his name. "The synagogue, yes, that's right. As we indicated on the form. We have an architect, a plan, all we need is permission from you and we will begin construction immediately."

Hal may not have been prepared to be so directly involved in neighborhood conflict. The zoning board was usually a pretty quiet place, but now he was on the spot. "Well, sure, but acourse it isn't just up to me. We got a board here and all."

Blitz nodded as if his knowledge of village politics was extensive. "Naturally," he said. "I presume you'll need to vote on our proposal, is that right?"

Hal had recovered now and sat back in his chair. "After we've had a chance to discuss it and gotten some community input, then we vote, you're right about that."

Blitz nodded. "And when might we expect that to occur? I rather thought the vote might take place tonight."

But before Hal could answer, someone in the back shouted out, "What about the traffic?"

Blitz jerked in his chair as if he'd been shot, but Hal was on the job. He looked toward the speaker and said, "That ain't Mr. Blatz' problem, Jim. It's just like any other construction in the village, streets blocked off and the like."

"Yeah, except it's permanent maybe."

Now Blitz turned and spoke. "I gather the concern is that our community is growing and there may be more joining us, especially if we have a new building with better facilities." He turned back to Hal. "Mr. Chairman, I think this is a legitimate concern. After all, this is a small neighborhood, sheltered before now from anything other than controlled growth. I can tell you that we intend to be very sensitive to this issue, I can assure you of that. I have, however, spoken to my colleagues at Christ Presbyterian, just to the east of us, and they informed me that approval of their expansion occurred in a matter of days. Is there some reason this seems to be more complicated?"

The question seemed to upset Hal who looked anxiously left and right for someone to help out because everyone knew what the delay was about, why it took longer for Jews to be approved than Presbyterians, even if no one was going to say so directly. The audience seemed to respond to the sudden tension in the room, a low murmur was emitted from somewhere, and people looked away in embarrassment. Whatever might be their secret thoughts, or even the truth, everyone in our neighborhood liked to think of himself as being a good neighbor, friendly, open to new ideas and suggestions from others. It was a protective illusion that allowed us to feel better about ourselves, though in this case it was in part the clannishness of the Jews that encouraged introspection. Had they made an effort some might say to get to know us, if they were friendlier, maybe more accepting, then we wouldn't even be here. But we didn't know these people, and it was clear they didn't want to know us.

In this room with the seats small enough for younger bodies, no one was going to make any overt display of animosity, but Hal apparently felt the potential was there for an ugly scene. He looked down at the rabbi and said decisively, "Every case's different, Mr. Blatz. Everyone's unique. But our board meets again in a month, and I can guarantee you we'll have a decision by then.

Blitz stood as if to protest this further delay but Hal gaveled the meeting to a close and the room emptied in a hurry until it was only Blitz and a collection of his followers standing in the front, their black hats and babushkas bobbing rhythmically, as they talked among themselves, though to what purpose it was impossible to guess.

The next morning small groups of people gathered on street corners with kids and dogs surrounding them, talking about what happened at the school. Strangely, if one had expected residual resentment to boil up, the opposite was more the case, as if approaching nearer the enemy and inspecting them had the effect of robbing people of their outrage. As a result of the meeting, the strange was no longer as strange as before.

"Tell the truth, I was embarrassed," Charlie Schmitz said. "Who the hell are we to say they can't build an addition to their church? That rabbi was right. When the Presbyterians wanted to put a new hall on there no one said a word."

"Synagogue," Dottie Adams said. "They call it a synagogue, not a church."

"Yeah," Ed said. "Well, whatever, we got no business mucking around in the whole thing. They seem like good people, with their families, their kids and now they're making our houses worth more money. Something wrong with that? So they don't say hello if you see them on the street, so what? Can you tell me a reason we should give a good goddamn? What's more, I like going over to that little deli they got over there in the strip mall. You ever try that pastrami? Beats the hell out of a sub sandwich, I'll tell you that right now."

And while the meeting at the school might not have seemed the ideal vehicle to transmit feeling, Yakov Blitz' followers also seemed marginally friendlier. They also had dogs to be walked, and women would now wave shyly as they passed our houses often accompanied by children.

On one occasion Sandy and I were standing at our posts at the mailbox when a couple passed by and nodded in our direction. "Fiddler on the Roof," she said again and it occurred to me that if she were going to choose an alternative reality the position of the Jews in nineteenth century Russia might mimic her present situation, limited and yet not without room to maneuver.

As much as anything, though, it could have been the image of Yakov Blitz standing in the well of the auditorium asserting his rights that turned people around and then only because his frustration with the process seemed real and understandable. We simply want to go our own way, he seemed to say, even if that's different from yours. In the days and weeks that followed there seemed no reasonable way to oppose this.

The building permit was approved by the zoning board without discussion at their next meeting and construction on the new wing of the synagogue began soon afterwards. When the framing was finished, we received another circular, this one on synagogue letterhead inviting the neighborhood to an oneg Shabbat after services on Friday to consecrate the new building.

That night most of us gathered in the shadow of the partly-completed edifice which was blessed in turn by the pastors of the Presbyterian and Baptist churches before Yakov Blitz offered a Hebrew prayer no one understood. Then he turned to the group and said, "We extend a warm welcome to our friends in this small community. We hope to be better neighbors in the future. Torah instructs us to be accommodating to all strangers. In that spirit we invite you not to be strangers here."

I looked up at the wire encircling the neighborhood that had started everything. It was still there but seemed less threatening than before. It made the eruv more noticeable than before, and the wire's harsh and forbidding aspect was leavened by bits of toilet paper that remained.

What had started as an artificial boundary meant to provide the faithful a means to live more easily with God's requirements had the unintended effect of including within it others who had no desire to be part of their community. Like any existing authority, people in the neighborhood hadn't welcomed a challenge, especially the one offered by Yakov Blitz. And it wouldn't be over anytime soon. If a fragile peace had been affected through the school meeting and the oneg, there was no way to say whether it would hold if more of us sold our houses and were replaced by Blitz' faithful. The children of the orthodox still didn't play with ours and if we weren't exactly the Jets and the Sharks, it was pretty clear that there would be little social mixing in the neighborhood. Tonight, everyone was making nice, but in this, as in most things, there is a tipping point. Everyone was relieved that conflict had been avoided, that the new addition had been built, but we'd have to see what it brought in the way of more problems. In the cool night air with people circulating, drinking tea, and smiling at one another beneath the encircling wire no one seemed very interested in predictions for the future.

UTKATASANA MEANS INTENSE
IN SANSKRIT

Things were getting weird in the neighborhood. The older people, who had moved here for more affordable new homes in the Seventies were seeing changes no one had foreseen and while it gave them plenty to talk about down at the supermarket, they weren't happy. First there had been the establishment of an eruv, a sequestered district for the orthodox Jews, in Greengate, followed by the new synagogue their rabbi built. Then we heard about the passion parties in which eager young women sold sex toys in quiet living rooms to neighborhood housewives who probably had no idea what a thong was but wanted one just the same. Looking out my window, I could see Mormon boys in white shirts and black pants circling the block on bicycles looking ceaselessly for converts. In the midst of all this, new people were arriving even as others moved on or went into residential treatment. Change was in the air.

But everything else paled in comparison to the impact of the new yoga center which had moved into the old Arby's space in the shopping center and was drawing converts in tights and scoop necked jerseys to its classes every day. Posters were pinned to trees all over the neighborhood, outraging the environmentalists among us, and just reading the descriptions was a new adventure in Sanskrit. According to the flyers, the Center offered Hatha, Vinyasa, something called Kundalini that sounded more like calisthenics than anything else, plus Iyengar, Power Yoga, and Tantra, which was supposed to increase your sex drive. The gossip was that some of the people from the passion parties were doubling up over at the yoga center, but it was hard to know.

There was Thermal yoga which was held in a room heated to 110 degrees and even a class in what they were calling yogic flying that involved throwing yourself off the ground while meditating in the lotus position. Whether it was realistic to think people like us could actually propel ourselves off a mat was questionable, but it was the yoga center itself that people reacted to. To some, this seemed like going too far by the rather limited standards of our community but judging from the jammed parking lot in front of the building a lot of people were coming by out of curiosity, if nothing else. Meanwhile new notices were going up on the community bulletin board in Safeway inviting newcomers to come in for free introductory classes and a cup of green tea.

"I like tits as much as the next guy," Joe Shelton told me one day down at the Coffee Stop. "But some of these women just shouldn't be dressing that way. It don't leave a single thing to the imagination and with some of them I don't even want to imagine it."

This was as thoughtful a comment as I'd ever heard from Joe, but his opinion made no impression on the new yogis in our neighborhood. And since the adherents of the art tended to be affluent, area storeowners who had despaired of drawing new business during the recession were hard at work developing marketing plans for the newcomers, whether their businesses had anything to do with yoga or not.

Namaste Bail Bonds, which was only in the neighborhood in the first place because of our proximity to the courthouse, was an obvious example, though it was hard to see the relationship between perfect peace and doing hard time in prison. But there were other outfits like Savasana Subs and Smoothies, featuring an herbal tea concoction guaranteed to increase your potency and t-cell production. The Korean cleaners, who had cleverly offered a special on Beaver Hats and gabardine cloaks for the orthodox Jews, now featured a line of non-stick mats made of bamboo along with tights and bolsters in a variety of colors. And Safeway had organized a new aisle devoted to energy bars and vitamin drinks.

Which could have been the extent of yoga's impact on our community. It might have been a small sensation like the free lunch come-ons at the steak house held by investment companies eager to lock up whatever retirees had set aside or the bus outings to Cripple Creek and Blackhawk where girls in leotards lured in white-haired suckers with promises of loose slots and ample buffets. "I know the slots those old goats are interested in," Dory Samson commented one day, "but those girls are too smart to fall for that."

The yoga center was different, in part because it promised nothing and gave little away. It simply existed, waiting for the faithful to come in for their morning dose of exhilaration, and it turned out they didn't have to wait long. The yoga teachers were not only younger and better looking than any of the women in the neighborhood, but with paradoxical modesty implicitly claimed a higher level of consciousness and displayed little self-doubt. This was a draw in itself since I'd always assumed doubt went along with breathing as a natural element of life.

Whatever the reason for the attraction, I was surprised to answer the bell one morning and see Joe Shelton dressed in tight shorts and wearing a headband on my front porch. When I greeted him and remarked on his outfit, Joe said "You can put shit on me all you want but there's something going on over there. It's deep."

It was hard to know exactly what Joe might mean by this, but I hadn't seen him up before noon in years. He tended to hole up in his house reading old issues of National Geographic, often emerging late at night to pick up his mail or walk his dog, before the dog died.

Joe was not someone I knew well, though we'd been neighbors for ten years. Much of what I did know of him was neighborhood legend about how he'd been a high school football star, went off to school in the East, received an MBA from Wharton and then came home to marry his high school sweetheart with whom he'd produced four kids in short order and moved into the nicest house in the area. What came after that was unclear, though the word was that his wife had left abruptly without even a note. I'd once seen a sign for "Shelton Realty" in his basement when we were playing ping pong but there were no listings that I knew of and as far as I could tell Joe had no office and never went to work. The rumor was that he'd inherited money which would explain his ability to hold onto the house but not the fact that it was now a ramshackle remnant of its former glory. An entire wall was lined with Dr. Pepper cans, and all three floors were littered with bags of pretzels and corn curls over discarded newspapers. In fact, what was true of the house was true of Joe, who if he had ever been an athlete, showed no evidence of it now. It had good bones but had fallen into disrepair. Which brought us back to yoga.

It was clear Joe wasn't alone in his new-found adherence. Women I'd known for years were walking around the neighborhood in brightly colored tights talking with enthusiasm about their chakras and even a cynic would admit there'd been an overall improvement in posture. Some understandable confusion went along with this as when Maureen Morris bowed and said "Namaste" as she walked past our house with her schnauzer, but she obviously meant well so I said Namaste in return. Why not? Who did it hurt?

If Yoga had brought a new sense of purpose to Greengate, the practitioners had a messianic gleam in their eyes which some found objectionable for its implied suggestion that they were in possession of a truth that had eluded the rest of us. But this was unfair. You would have seen the same expression a decade earlier if you'd encountered a marathon runner at a party who eschewed alcohol for vegetable juice and occasionally dropped into a long calf stretch in the middle of a sentence. Yoga, like running, appealed to the middle-class illusion that life was not really half over if only we could find the right formula to make us more beautiful and live forever. For those who were around the first turn in life with gray hair and middle-aged spread this could be narcotic. Illusion, after all, is essential as are new preoccupations. Without them, there would be nothing to love and argue about, and life would quickly become overrun with monotony.

What might have made yoga different was the sense that rather than just being therapeutic it was its own ministry. There was a teacher or leader in every class, but they always emphasized that they knew no more than anyone else about the true path. This being so I shouldn't have been surprised that morning to see Joe Shelton demanding that I accompany him to the studio. Yoga was like romance. When you were in love you wanted everyone you knew to be in love as well. Joe was in love.

I protested that I didn't have the right equipment. But Joe would have none of it. "What equipment?" he said. "You got a pair of shorts, right? You got a water bottle? That's all the equipment you're going to need."

This seemed to settle any objections I might have had and fifteen minutes later Joe and I joined twenty other people in a small, overheated room at the yoga center. The air was humid; someone had been burning incense and music that reminded me vaguely of Ravi Shankar was playing on the large speakers. In fact, the whole scene channeled the Sixties including the blissed-out looks on the faces of those around me, which I found unsettling.

On the wall was a cardboard plaque with a heading that said, "Yogic Wisdom." Below this there was ornate lettering that read: "Go back to that state of pure being, where the "I am" is still in its purity before it got contaminated with "this I am" or "that I am." This was attributed to someone named Sri Ramana Mahari.

Other than Sri Mahari's message, the walls were bare leaving open whether the decoration was incomplete or had been abandoned. Even the Yogic Wisdom sign had an accidental look about it, though it was framed and mounted and seemed to demand our attention.

Most of the people in the class sat on their mats in a kind of controlled stupor apparently waiting for direction, but one hotshot in black tights and an attitude ponytail was standing on his head and bicycling his legs to get warmed up, which wouldn't have taken much in this room.

I nodded at him and raised my eyebrows. "That's Seth," Joe said. "Major asshole. He's in teacher training. Pisses me right off." Then he dropped into child's pose and said nothing more.

Before long the teacher came in, working her way around the studio like a talk show host, bowing to one and all and wiggling her fingers to those on the other side of the room. I was relieved to see she was not one of the nubile goddesses I'd seen walking around the shopping center but instead looked past forty with a blonde top knot and a small pot belly that made me like her. She bowed again and intoned "Namaste" in a sepulchral voice, which the class returned with avidity. Then she raised her arms as if in a salute to an unseen god and intoned "It is with great love and compassion that we begin this practice of yoga."

Being literal minded I wondered if "this practice" referred to today's class or to yoga in general but everyone else seemed oblivious to any ambiguity. I looked over at Joe, expecting an ironic comment, but he was standing in prayer position, hands before his chest, eyes closed. What followed was first some breathing exercises and then a series of asanas with interesting animal names like dog, rabbit, snail, even snake and tortoise, all of which the teacher translated into Sanskrit as if it were her native language. It was hard to know whether anything she was saying was accurate since everything seemed to be banda or nanda, nonsense syllables to me, but I sensed some comfort in our shared ignorance of this tradition. What's more you had to feel it gave the teacher an aura of authenticity, no matter what she might actually be saying.

As we moved through the poses, the teacher enumerated the many benefits of doing yoga, from curing flatulence to improving thyroid function and digestion. Even so, when we were in "wind-releasing pose" a quiet susurrus of farting went through the room that no one seemed to mind or even register. "Breathe and relax," the teacher said. "Relax and breathe." And so, we did.

There was a kind of blind obedience to the commands intoned from the front of the room and periodically the teacher would move to adjust someone's hand or foot right or left, while giving the rest of us directions that seemed impossible to follow. "Turn your inner thighs out as you flatten your belly and exhale into your groins," she said at one point. "Spiral your outside elbows," she added, but before I could even understand these directions, we were on to something else that was equally impossible.

At the end, everyone sat on their mats and meditated while the teacher intoned "Om" over and over for fifteen minutes. Finally, we were released into the outer lobby where members of the class milled around in sweaty fulfillment and drank green tea from an urn. Seth was surrounded by several admiring women, but Joe held himself aloof until the teacher came out. She walked over, put her hand on Joe's shoulder and looked directly into my eyes. "Won't you introduce me to your friend, Joseph?"

I'd never heard anyone call him Joseph before, but Joe seemed to stand straighter now, beaming at the attention. Introductions were made and that's how I met Margo Adler and came to understand something about how she had built a following and would be an agent of change in Joe's life. But that was later.

The common life of a community is fragile. It's received wisdom that people in the suburbs are less sophisticated than those in cities. We do well to remember though that an early proponent of the whole idea was none other than Frank Lloyd Wright, who saw in the leafy suburbs of Chicago a respite from the chaos men faced when they drove into work every day. I doubt that anyone in our neighborhood has ever heard of Wright, but that's not important. Our community is small and self-selected, but there are recognized leaders, generally accepted values and an idea of what makes life worthwhile. Simple things: Mow your grass, wave when a car passes by, show up for Pride Day to help spruce up the entrance and exit from the neighborhood, rules the orthodox Jews broke with alacrity as they were obedient to a higher authority.

I've never actually participated in Pride Day and seldom attend holiday parties. No one seems to hold that against me, perhaps because I pay my Homeowners Association dues. Who knows? People here smile to hide private pain, try to raise their children well, nod at the stories of others whether they're interesting or not and generally practice tolerance, up to a point. That is, we tend to tolerate the eccentricities of others who are essentially like us. There are bad marriages, children who fail, people who drink too much, occasional instances of adultery announced by raised voices and the destruction of crockery. If it's kept behind a tight veil of discretion no one says a thing. Stan Freeman's despair is no one else's business; neither is Ted Hillman's drinking or the fact that Jim Sherman has been out of work for a year and lives on the largesse of his mother-in-law, who doesn't like him. Everyone knows these things, but they're seldom discussed or alluded to, except among friends on the back patio after dinner on summer evenings when everyone's drunk too much wine.

Stability enables us to accept change and despite everything that has happened lately no one in Greengate is putting a sign on his lawn and leaving. Even if the yoga center was reaching out aggressively in its passive way, intruding in our lives to a greater extent than some would like, it was hard to see why its existence should be any more noteworthy than the health classes down at the YMCA that some of the men still went to daily.

Without any overt agreement, Joe began stopping by three mornings a week for Margo Adler's nine o'clock class which seemed to draw other middle-aged people, though no one you'd really call old. Joe was always pushing to get there early so he could claim a favorite spot, on the right side of the room in the second row, with a clear view of both the mirrors and Margo. "There's a woman who goes in the front who's got a great ass," he said in explanation.

With all the bending and down dogs, it seemed there was little opportunity to admire others, or so I thought, but Joe was adamant. "Check it out," he said. "I'm serious."

"You might just introduce yourself," I said. "Get to know her."

"I don't want to know her," Joe said. "I just want to watch her. Why ruin a good thing?"

I didn't really see what was good about this, especially since I knew he hadn't had a date since his wife left. "Does she wear a wedding band?"

Joe shook his head. "But that don't mean anything. Half of them put their jewelry away when they come in the door."

I nodded, though I hadn't noticed one way or the other. Then Margo entered the studio and class began. She bowed her way around the room, and we started with deep breathing, as we always did. You wouldn't think people would need to learn to breathe but Margo said that without breathing yoga was just a lot of stretching. It seemed like stretching to me anyway, but Margo had a quiet intensity that compelled attention as she corrected this person or encouraged that one, while trying to make sure we were getting that special growl in the back of the throat that she liked and few of us were ever able to perfect.

Looking around, I noticed the room had filled since Joe and I came in. Directly behind me was a woman I assumed must be from the eruv since she was dressed in black, had a kerchief on her head and wore a full skirt and leggings despite the heat. I looked at her in what I hoped was a friendly way, but her eyes were opaque and uninterested. It was as if I wasn't there.

A neighborhood is nothing more than a loose assortment of people drawn together by living arrangements they've made at random. On the surface there's nothing about this that would remotely suggest that people who live in proximity to one another should be more than acquaintances cooperating in the odd problems involving fences or sewer lines. Yet in Greengate there are expectations with positive value placed on being more than superficially friendly or helpful. We're governed by these quiet commands and so for years there had been communal concern about Joe Shelton living alone with no friends or family nearby. People made dark suggestions regarding his state of mind or worried that he might drink himself to death or worse.

This being so, you'd think people would welcome Joe's new interest in yoga or in anything. The reverse is what actually occurred. There was general suspicion about his new enthusiasm as if he'd betrayed some article of faith. People had grown comfortable with the idea of Joe being pathetic and lost, in need of help, an object of concern.

"What's wrong with that old fool, prancing around in his underwear like that?" Sherry Hacker asked one morning at coffee. It would have been rude to bring up Sherry's sponsorship of a passion party the month before, especially since she was not alone among the women in the neighborhood with this particular interest. But things got much worse when Jenny Chambers noticed a red pick-up parked in Joe's driveway one morning.

"I don't know how long it's been there," Jenny said. "But when I turned off the light after Jimmy last night, it was there and it's still there now."

In our neighborhood people often refer to celebrities by their first names as if they might just turn up at Oktoberfest one year, but Jenny wasn't the only one keeping an eye on Joe's house. Jane Dorsey, the unofficial mayor of the block, was on the job and reported in breathless tones the next day that the truck "belongs to that yoga teacher over to the strip mall." This was mildly surprising given the transparently spiritual nature of Margo's presentation in class but no doubt yoga instructors have needs too.

But if it was true that Joe and Margo were keeping company, you'd never know it from Joe, who whatever other faults he might have had, was not one to kiss and tell. Early comment regarding the couple was always prefaced by "Of course it's really none of my business," but since people in Greengate actually had no business to attend to beside their interest in others, this was largely ignored. It's remarkable how often people, when given a chance to be gracious, choose not to be.

Time went by. Seasons changed, children went through the slow process of maturation, three more men on our block lost their jobs and two houses were sold at auction at prices below market, upsetting people nearly as much as the fact that the houses were snapped up by orthodox Jewish families, one of whom had seven children. I got busy with one thing and another and months went by without my having visited the yoga center. Then one morning, as if he'd been sent by providence, there was Joe again, standing on my front porch. The difference was striking. His posture had improved and he had slimmed down, but more than this there was what could only be called an expression of sincerity on his face that I didn't recognize.

"Get your stuff," he said without explaining himself further. "Class is in fifteen."

This time the dynamic in the room had changed, though Margo was still in front going on about our chakras and the ways in which various asanas would improve the functioning of the thymus gland or move our digestive systems in more productive ways. For all the good it may do, there's a lot of bullshit associated with yoga, and you just have to go with it. Margo was so earnest in her beliefs that they were easy to tolerate, at least in her. And who could say with absolute certainty that she was wrong? I hadn't known about the seven chakras before meeting her so for me the learning curve was steep.

When we entered the room, Joe took his place in front facing the mirror with Margo directly to his left and Seth flanking him. Joe still couldn't do handstands, but his improved flexibility was impressive. The rest of us formed rows in the center and back of the room. Everything was organized around Margo and her two admirers.

A woman on the mat next to mine leaned over and said, "I saw you come in with Joseph. Are you friends?"

I nodded. "We live on the same block."

"He's such a dedicated yogi," the woman said.

I was getting used to people calling him Joseph but the idea of his being a yogi was new. "Do you come here often?" I asked.

"Two or three times a week," she said. "Not like them." She indicated Joe and Seth who were orchestrating rather different stretches as if they were contrapuntal elements of the same video. "Joseph's starting teacher training" she confided sotto voce.

This surprised me. "Really? Joe's going to be a yoga teacher?"

The woman nodded. "He'll be wonderful, I think, so sensitive. But it's such a commitment."

I considered this. I had always assumed people like Margo just took some classes and started doing it. In my mind, it was like the old medical school idea: watch one, do one, teach one. But apparently there was more to it than that with yoga. Maybe they traveled to India to sit at the feet of wise, experienced swamis, studied Sanskrit, steeped themselves in the culture. Who could say for sure? It just wasn't the way I was accustomed to seeing my friend.

I wondered why Joe had come by for me this morning, why he wanted to involve me in the class again. Perhaps to show how much he had changed, to validate his new life with someone who'd known him before yoga. It could have been as simple as an expression of pride in what he'd accomplished. It was hard to say. But in that hot room, watching him move with sure confidence through the poses, I had an insight: transformation was always problematical, never easy, and much of what passed for concern about Joe in the neighborhood was really poorly disguised envy.

Beyond that was the experience of yoga itself, the quiet but insistent claim it seemed to make on the lives of its adherents, the suggestion that life could be more, that a higher level of consciousness was within your grasp, that your body need not shrink and shrivel with onrushing age, that your digestive and reproductive systems could revive, that in general you could achieve a level of well-being unimagined before. Had I doubted this, Joe confided in me as we were going to class.

"You wouldn't believe the hardons I'm getting now," he said. "I threw away that Viagra and the Prozac. I just don't need that shit now that I got yoga."

I didn't necessarily think this was evidence of personal growth and it occurred to me that Joe might not be giving Margo the credit she deserved. But something had obviously shifted in him. Watching the obvious pride he took in being a leader in this setting was if not inspirational, at least touching, even as I wondered whether it would collapse of its own weight as quickly as it had appeared. Even if this were true, however, Joe had achieved something he hadn't possessed previously and that was what mattered.

We moved slowly through the asanas with Margo accompanying our movements with solemn murmurs in Sanscrit: Dhamasana, Ushtasana, Garudasana and then my personal favorite Utkatasana or "Powerful Pose." Finally, we arrived at Siddhasana or corpse pose, which supposedly delivered you to a perfectly stilled mind. I wasn't there yet, but no doubt this was due to my own imperfections.

Joe appeared to be well along on the journey to perfect peace. Of course, it was the way I wanted to see him, a man who had been stuck in the detritus of a failed life for much too long made whole by divine yogic intervention. He had taken the ruined house, the spent fortune, and the old, yellowed magazines and turned them into love, life, perhaps something approaching wisdom. You had to like it for him.

As I left the little building and entered the busy parking lot, a smell of saffron was in the air, and for that moment I imagined a scene with barefoot priests in robes moving around rather than housewives in huge SUVs. I remembered Sri Mahari and his injunction to go back to that state of pure being, where the "I am" is still in its purity, yogic wisdom. It was somewhat problematical to accept the dumpy Margo as being an agent of change rather than merely Joe's new girlfriend, but if there was anything the various religious traditions agreed on it was that God appeared to us in various forms and disguises, so who could say for sure?

Our neighborhood was fluid, moving, dynamic, adjusting to changes of one kind or another just as all of us did in our personal lives. So we'd absorbed the yoga center and whatever it had to teach and show us. For that moment in the crowded parking area, this seemed like a lot. Certainty was no doubt doomed to fade as quickly as it had appeared, but regardless of that something had happened. Was it, as Joe said, something deep? It would take time to know for sure, but it wasn't impossible.

RENTAL

There are 483 houses in Greengate, one of which is being torn down and another in the process of being rebuilt. It is a way of convincing ourselves that we're a dynamic community, growing and changing, always new, despite the age of the homes and mature vegetation that surrounds us. Of these houses, 482 are occupied by their owners and one is a rental, having been purchased by the son and daughter-in-law of Bob Monroe after Bob's wife died and he decided to move to a condo near the University. No one's actually asked Bob's kids about this, but the scuttlebutt is that they got the house at a sweetheart price and consider it an "investment," though what this means to them is a mystery. The house has increased in value three times since Bob moved out but still his kids hold on to it as a rental.

Initially, this situation raised some anxiety in neighbors, particularly when a black family responded to the "For Rent" sign on the lawn. Everyone breathed a collective sigh of relief when the black family moved on, and a single mother named Sally Parini moved in with her two children and live-in lover who was rumored to be the father of at least one of the kids. While there was general appreciation that Sally wasn't black, there was no move to embrace or befriend her due to a Greengate prejudice against renters. Sally wasn't listed in the neighborhood directory or included in the twice-yearly neighborhood parties and the explanation I got from Liz Willman was "I don't consider someone who's renting to be part of the community, right?"

I didn't argue but didn't really understand since before coming to Greengate I'd lived most of my life in apartments in the city and had never previously owned a house. But I was plainly an outlier. The community reaction to there being a rental house in Greengate might have been expressed by Stan Miles who said one day, "Black, white trash, don't make no difference so far as I can see. You ask me, they're about the same. Here one day, gone the next, probably in the middle of the night."

Of course, Sally would not have agreed with Stan's description. Who wants to be described as white trash? But she seemed to have a chip on her shoulder owing to complaints others made about her having parties that left three or four cars parked out on the street for a couple of days and her garbage cans remaining out on her lawn long after they'd been emptied on trash day.

I didn't know Sally well since she lived around the corner on an adjacent street, but I'd seen her from time to time while walking in the Arboretum. Once when I was wearing my school sweatshirt she stopped and asked if I'd gone to Yale, volunteering that she had.

"Boola boola," I said, not knowing what else to say. It was a long time ago, another life really and another wife. I was in touch with neither these days and didn't miss them. Sally stood there expectantly waiting for me to answer so I just nodded in affirmation. She didn't really look like what I thought of as an Ivy League type with her red dreadlocks and pierced lips, but who knows these days? Then she told me she was a "craniosacral therapist."

I responded with what I thought of as the interested questioning look that had gotten me through high school French. Sally sighed with the kind of tolerance one reserves for children and idiots. Then she said, "We reject that western medicine bullshit that just wants to get people sick and keep them that way. It's like sacred touch therapy to stimulate membranes and get the nervous system back where it's supposed to be. My practice is also into wellness and alternative healing methods. You know massage, herbs, acupuncture, all that."

"Cool," I said, just to say something, but Sally acted as if I'd expressed skepticism about modern healing methods.

"It works," she said, jutting her jaw out, eyes blazing. "I've got some testimonials from patients on it I can give you. If you read them, you might learn about something other than the propaganda you get in this society."

I passed on the articles, but when I mentioned the conversation to my wife, a physician, she was amused. "Got to stay away from western medicine," she said. "It might actually do some good."

It had nothing to do with her, but our friend Audrey, also a doctor, was insulted when I told her about my conversation with Sally. It turned out Audrey was involved in alternative medicine somehow. "She's a fraud," Audrey said dismissively. "Sacred touch, my ass. She gives back rubs, for Christ's sake, maybe with a happy ending. I talked to her about it once."

"She says she went to Yale," I responded, not meaning to defend Sally.

"Yale, right," Audrey said. "She could have spent a weekend there once, bought the sweatshirt. Maybe she has a Yale lock."

Audrey had a knowing air about her that was often convincing, but she was sometimes a little careless with her facts. "And how do you know this?"

"I just know, all right," Audrey said heatedly. "Jesus!"

I decided to let it drop there, having pissed off enough women for one day but what Sally had said interested me. Who couldn't use a little sacred touch, whatever that was, whether it really did anything for you or not?

In the morning, I often walk with my friend Joe Simonson, a tall thin man, who along with his wife Sondra make up the only inter-racial couple on our block. Joe is fond of philosophical observations, though he eschews intellectuals and is proud of the fact that he never graduated from college. He might be similar to Eric Hoffer or one of the stevedore poets, a man who takes pride in his pithy everyday observations. Like Audrey, Joe has the gift of certainty and often begins sentences with "You probably never thought of this" and then stands back waiting for the shocked reaction to brilliance he expects. Joe lives across the street from Sally, facing the Park and has had the opportunity to study her comings and goings at greater lengths than I have. Returning from our walk one morning, he indicated several cars parked on the street in front of Sally's house.

"Do you know how much that one is worth?" Joe asked, indicating a red sedan I hadn't noticed.

"I have no idea."

"$100,000 if it's a nickel," Joe said. "Must be a customer with a lot of jack. And that's not the only one I've seen out there. Personal services, know what I mean?"

I wasn't sure what point he was making about the car, especially since there was also a refrigerator with a broken door sitting on the lawn along with a movable basketball hoop and a couple of broken lounge chairs. I remembered Audrey's skepticism about Sally's medical practice. "You think she's a hooker?" I asked. This would be new and interesting considering the rest of the neighborhood.

"One hundred per cent," Joe said. "And this isn't the first time this guy has been around, trust me on that."

I immediately felt imperceptive as I often did around Joe who had apparently been keeping a log of Sally's visitors. "She told me she's a therapist," I said. "Sacred touch."

Joe smiled. "Exactly," he said knowingly and winked.

"Good to know," I said. Then, quickly so as not to give the wrong impression, "Not that it has anything to do with me."

"Of course not," Joe said. "Not my point. In a way, though, it's logical."

"I don't follow you" I said. "We're in the suburbs, not down on Colfax."

"Not in that way, but it's like a metaphor. She rents her house, and then they rent her by the hour or however long, like a hot sheet motel. Doesn't that make sense?"

Joe was a deep thinker, and this wasn't the first time he'd seen connections between things that escaped me. I looked over at Sally's nondescript yard. There was a slight scent of smoke in the air along with the sweet smell of rotting garbage, but no people.

"That's not really fair, is it? I mean, they're just cars. Maybe she has a lot of friends. Anyway, don't we all rent ourselves for periods in a sense, when we go to work and get paid for the hours we put in, or when my wife sees patients at her office?"

"This isn't your wife, Man. And it isn't Audrey. Think about it," Joe said, and walked back toward his house.

Sally was a tall redhead with a nice figure, but not really seductive. In any case, she didn't seem to me like the kind of woman who'd be entertaining men as Joe suggested in her home. Still, the suggestion that we had a sexual professional operating a brothel in Greengate gave a different slant to the neighborhood, there was no denying that.

When I got inside the house, I told my wife what Joe had said about the expensive cars. "Sure," she said. "You didn't know this? I mean, touch? Massages? Get serious."

"You did?"

"I'm late for work," my wife replied.

So, there you were. To hear Sally tell it, she was a medical professional with a Yale degree, working hard to support her kids as a single mother. She went to work, came home, saw her kids and her friends, nothing wrong with that. Her yard was a mess, and she didn't mix well with others in Greengate, but neither did the Jews in their erev. From what I read in the papers, the fact that she had a couple of kids out of wedlock wasn't extraordinary in the current climate and for what that was worth, the guy who had moved in with her was apparently their father. Why they never married was a mystery but what of it?

In a community where making judgments about others was supposedly frowned upon, gossip about Sally was rife. You could say people in Greengate had a lot of time on their hands to speculate about their neighbors and there was definitely a bias in favor of those who fit a certain pattern. People who didn't fit, whether they were Jews, blacks, gay or, in Sally's case, renters, came in for special scrutiny. For no reason, I went on the Yale website and found that a Sally Parini had not only attended the

University but graduated with a degree in romance languages. This didn't seem to have much to do with Sally's current career, but changing jobs is common these days. I decided to cut Sally some slack and assume the best about her and her menagerie.

While I was on my sabbatical from Sally there was a crime spree of sorts in our community, at least that was the way it appeared on "Nextdoor," which reported each incident with breathtaking accuracy. Someone had stolen a car, another had their mail taken out of their box, as indeed we had the year before, a group of strange boys was wandering around a neighborhood, and others were racing cars at night on Hampden Avenue. More significant was the growing number of thefts of catalytic converters out of cars parked in the street. A few houses were broken into while people were out of town or even during daylight when the occupants were at work. Whether this was due to the economic downturn hitting the country or simple boredom on the part of teenagers was unclear. Whatever the true cause, the growth of crime was the reason I next had contact with Sally.

She showed up at my door one morning in a revealing tank top and a short skirt. Before I could even say hello, she walked into the vestibule and said, "They stole my goddamned car."

"Who?" I said, thinking maybe it had been one of the neighbors who disapproved of her exposed garbage cans.

"I don't know fucking who," Sally said. "Right out of my damned driveway. It's just gone."

For no reason, I looked up and down the street as if I'd

see something that had eluded her but there was nothing there. "Sorry to hear that," I said.

"Yeah, right," Sally said. "Bummer. So give me a ride to work."

Not would you give me a ride to work but a kind of command that I do so. I looked toward the kitchen, hoping my wife would rescue me but she had left early for her office, and I was alone. Beyond this, I couldn't see why Sally had asked me rather than one of her closer neighbors. Maybe it was that Yale connection. "Work?" I said stupidly.

"Yeah," Sally said. "I've got a life, appointments, patients, you know."

Why this had become my problem was unclear, but I could see there was no point in raising questions of logic with her. "Okay," I said. "I'll get my jacket."

Given her appearance, I might have expected Sally to say she had to change, but when I came back, she was standing in the same place, arms crossed impatiently around her breasts, ready to go. I didn't know how a craniosacral therapist was expected to dress, but I wasn't going to find out from Sally. She showed a lot of leg getting into my car but didn't seem self-conscious about this either. "Let's go," she said. "I'm late already."

Sally's office was in a squat blond building on Leetsdale adjacent to a shopping center which housed a Subway, Fantastic Sam's, Beltway tuxedos, Starbucks, Arthur Murray dance studio and for the less affluent a Goodwill supercenter. Whether there was any cross-over from these businesses with Sally's clientele was uncertain. Maybe after a hot dance lesson, people would need an adjustment or spinal treatment.

The ride down had been eerily quiet. Had I expected any small talk during the half hour drive, I would have been disappointed. Sally was on her phone the whole time, first calling the police to report the stolen car, then to her office saying she'd be late for her first patient. While she talked, I studied her surreptitiously, as was almost inevitable given that we were inches away from one another in the small car. Tendrils of hair curled down onto her neck and the tank top had moved forward revealing a semi-circle of her left breast with the suggestion of a nipple just adjacent. A small red heart was tattooed on her upper arm underneath which was printed "Hot stuff."

I come from a generation that held tattoos to be mildly disreputable, usually the product of a drunken night in the service that ended up in a down-at-the-heels tattoo parlor adjacent to whatever port bar you'd found. It was only recently that "body art" had become a sensation and now all sorts of people were sporting tattoos, including middle-aged businessmen I'd spotted at the gym with either Biblical psalms or messages similar to Sally's adorning their shoulders, backs or flanks. It was like wearing a bumper sticker on your skin, a way of communicating a belief or characteristic strongly held of which others might understandably be unaware.

I didn't say anything about this, however, and enjoyed the slight and unspoken sexual tension between us as we headed north through the city. When we got to the office, she got out of the car with no niceties and then leaned back in, her face set in a fixed smile. "I'm done around five, okay?" she said. And then she was gone.

Under normal circumstances, this could indicate that we were now friends or at least more than acquaintances.

It was the kind of thing I would have done for any neighbor in a similar situation. What made this day unusual was Sally's previous standoffishness, if not hostility, not just to me, but to Greengate as a whole. You might have thought she'd call an Uber or maybe some other friend even if she was pressed for time. The fact that she'd come to my house made me feel somewhere between a fall guy and a familiar face. Still, I couldn't have argued that I had anywhere else to be or that I was in thrall to a busy work schedule. Moreover, despite Sally's eccentricities, I suppose I was a little curious and pleased to be asked. I wanted to know about her. So, in the end I decided not to make too much of her brusque manner and headed back home. Perhaps by the evening she'd have rented a car or made other arrangements and wouldn't need me.

As it happened, however, Sally called just after five. "I'm done," she said. "I'll be in front whenever you get here."

"Maybe you should install a meter in your car," my wife said. "Who knows, this could turn into something, bring in real money. Anyway, where's the baby daddy? Why can't he give her a ride?"

I didn't know the answer to this, but it struck me that some wives might have been suspicious of their husbands driving attractive young women to and from work or maybe it was just that I would have liked it to bother my wife a little. In either case, she said nothing more except to ask me to pick up milk on my way back. Given the lack of interaction between Sally and me that morning, my wife may have been prescient, but it was a little discouraging to be that predictable.

Sally was outside her building after I fought the afternoon traffic to get back to the center of town yet while it had taken me forty minutes, she didn't display the slightest irritation with the delay. Of course, it was a free ride, a service I was performing, if you like, but some people might have been annoyed at having to wait.

"Tough day?" I said, just to say something, but again Sally acted as if her profession had been challenged.

"Every day's tough," she said. "Like, we see people who're sick, really need help, and a lot of them are on the rebound from traditional medicine, so we have to cure them from being cured by the so-called doctors they've seen before." She gestured with her arm as if an army of doctors in white coats had suddenly surrounded the car.

I didn't know if she was referring to my wife and Audrey but decided not to pick up on it. One tense person was enough. Before I could put the car in gear, however, Sally said, "Hey, want to come inside? I'll give you a freebie, you can see for yourself."

The first thought I had was in connection with Joe's assumption about the cars in front of Sally's house, but I was feeling reckless so followed her into her building. There was a deserted reception area in the front with a large sign on the wall that read, "Welcome to Your Good Health! We're glad you came!"

Sally beckoned me on, so I followed her through a warren of small offices that opened into a wider space with a cot and a chair next to it. No one else seemed to be in the office and Sally had now put on a yellow smock that could have been used by either artists or members of a bowling team but was apparently what she wore to work since there was an inscription on the pocket that read "Dr. Sally."

"Lie down," she ordered and took her place in the chair next to the bed.

I lay down feeling both a little anxious and stupid. I am not an especially adventurous person and live my life within a circumscribed space for the most part, but I was here and having come inside had little choice but to go along. Sally had lost her edge and was quite matter of fact now that she was in her element. When I was settled on the cot, she sat back and looked at me seriously examining me before diving into her method.

"Okay," she said. "The treatment is called Craniosacral because we're talking about the area between your cranium and sacrum, the lower end of your spinal cord. What I'm going to do is use touch to try to normalize your spinal cord and then manipulate the membranes and fluids around the cord to release the tension in your central nervous system, okay?"

Like most people who say okay frequently, it wasn't really a question, maybe a hope or a command. "I don't have any problems with my spinal cord," I said, feeling oddly criticized.

"That you know about," Sally corrected me. "In this fucked up society everyone's spinal cord gets turned around daily. It's inevitable."

This didn't seem like a clinical evaluation to me, but I was new to this, so I let it go. "Okay, you're right. No problems I know about with my spinal cord."

Sally nodded. Then she got down to work. She leaned over me and ran her hands first over my face rhythmically in a way that reminded me of Jewish women moving their arms in a circle while blessing candles on the sabbath, and then around my head and neck. She ran her fingers around the base of my skull and the small of my back, just above the coccyx. I couldn't remember the last time a woman I wasn't married to had massaged my ass, but this was curiously asexual. I was surprised how gentle she seemed, given her rather rough manner. Then Sally leaned back and closed her eyes as she held the opposite ends of what I guessed was my spine. Her eyelids fluttered and she seemed to mutter something like an incantation, though I couldn't make out what she said, maybe a prayer of some kind. Who knew?

While I didn't really believe Sally's mumbo jumbo about fluids and membranes, to my surprise, the muscles in my neck did begin to relax and a feeling of lightness replaced the chronic tension I felt in my forehead. I was aware of a soft vibration in my lower back, as if my spine was doing an internal rhumba and now my body went limp, gelatinous, as if Sally had somehow dissolved the bony parts and replaced them with soft tissue. Maybe this was the fluid she'd been talking about as now my body felt like the half-filled inner tubes we used to swim with at Willows Beach back in Madison.

It didn't matter. Whatever the cause, I was pinned to the bed, unable to move, forced to let go of whatever control I'd imagined I had over the situation. I was aware of a sharp acidic smell, rubbing alcohol maybe, but didn't remember it being applied before the treatment. Sally's eyes remained closed, her strong fingers providing warm pressure on my spine and back.

The procedure took less than fifteen minutes, but when Sally let go of my back and sat back, it was as if something had lifted me, and I was floating over the cot. I felt weightless for the first time I could remember. In time, this feeling released and I was able to sit on the side of the bed.

Sally took off the bowling shirt and hung it on a hook.

Then she said, "That's it. How did that feel?"

It's always interesting to watch a person do what she does professionally, even in the case of a profession my wife and Audrey claimed wasn't really a profession at all. I was impressed with Sally and saw her in a new way. "Amazing," I said, but Sally was unimpressed. She just nodded, modest now after the fact.

"If you had a longer treatment, it would be better," she said, as if pushing for more sessions. "I was just getting started."

"No doubt," I said. "But if you went on any longer, I'd probably have to spend the night here. I felt like I couldn't move from that bed."

We walked out of the building and started to drive home. Sally said, "They found the asshole who took the car. Well, not the asshole actually but at least the car. I'm having it towed home, so you won't have to drive me down here anymore."

I felt oddly disappointed at this though it made no sense having just been released from further chauffeur duty. "Is the car okay?"

Sally looked at me and smiled at the question. "How do I know? I haven't seen it yet, but it doesn't matter. I'll get it fixed and ready to go. I'll bet you're wondering why I didn't get Rick to drive me down here."

I supposed Rick was the lover, but I hadn't thought about him until my wife brought it up. "None of my business," I said. "I'm happy to help out."

"It's because he moved out a week ago," Sally said. "Actually, I kicked his ass out because he was pissing me off. Too clingy, hanging around all the time, calling five times a day when I was at work."

I nodded but there didn't seem to be much more to say. A life like hers was almost unimaginable to me, even if I'd been divorced and a single father for a while myself. There was an awkward silence after this until, almost as an afterthought, Sally said, "So what did you do all day? I mean I don't really know what you do."

"It's hard to explain," I said. "And not that interesting."

Sally laughed at this a loud hiccoughing laugh that made me like her more than I had before. "See," she said, when she caught her breath, "that makes it interesting. Everyone else tries to make out they're like this big heavy-hitter and exaggerate their own importance. You're the complete opposite. If what you said was a strategy, that would be killer. Come on, what do you do?"

I seldom had a chance to discuss my work with anyone, and I hadn't lied in saying it was hard for me to talk about, but suddenly something had changed in the air, and I felt comfortable even intimate with Sally in a way I wasn't with my other neighbors. I talked about economics and strategies of investing for a half-hour and when I dropped her off, she leaned over and kissed my cheek.

"Funny," she said, "I think you're a really interesting guy. Too bad you're married."

And before I could decide whether she'd just made a pass at me or not, Sally was out of the car and up the walk to her house.

When I went in and told my wife what had happened, she was unimpressed. "You're just suggestible," she said.

"What does that mean?"

"If she was a snake charmer or danced the Seven Veils, it would have the same effect," she said. "You'd come in and tell me how well it worked."

"And you know that how?"

"I've been married to you for twenty years," she said with a slight smile on her beautiful face. "I just know."

In ordinary circumstances, my day with Sally might have led to closer relations between us. We could have had her over for drinks, I might have met her for coffee, her kids might have mown my lawn and shoveled the sidewalk in winter, we could have exchanged funny notes from time to time or become Facebook friends. In fact, none of this happened. After the nearly accidental closeness of the ride down to her office and the intimacy of my craniosacral treatment, we retreated into our respective lives like shy lovers. We seldom spoke or even waved if we saw each other in the street. Part of this could have been due to my wife's tendency toward solitude but it was really the result of a kind of suburban alienation that never forces you to share an apartment hallway or a driveway with anyone else or interact at all with your neighbors unless a fence needs to be repaired or a lawn mower borrowed. Self-reliance has its limitations no matter what Emerson said. We are polite and friendly in a superficial way but seldom meet otherwise. This phenomenon is never spoken of in Greengate, but it is there, keeping us safely on our backyard patios all summer and inside in front of the fire in winter.

THE SHABBOS GOY

Long before I had even heard of Greengate, I lived with my mother in my grandfather's house in Northwest Denver. We had moved from Los Angeles after my father's early death, and I didn't need to be reminded that we were lucky to have been taken in. My grandfather was more devout than my parents had been and as a result, we become more religious as well, attending a conservative *shul* and observing not only all holidays but honoring the Sabbath as well.

Having no choice, I accepted these changes, but I always dreaded Saturdays. I disliked Saturday because it was the Sabbath and in my grandfather's home that meant a day of inactivity, a day on which I was expected to sit with my mother and grandparents in their comfortable North Side home and consider our places in God's great universe. I was not allowed to go outside and see my friends or watch a movie or even walk around the neighborhood. We couldn't turn on the television, listen to the radio or talk on the telephone. Neither was my mother allowed to cook or clean, which meant that after returning from morning services we all sat looking at nothing for five hours until the religious siege was lifted and life was allowed to continue.

This was in 1959 and I was in my freshman year at North High, a school populated somewhat unequally by Jews, blacks and Hispanics, all of whom jostled for room in the lunchroom as they did on the streets in our neighborhood. I had heard of other sections where Jews lived in Denver, areas with sumptuous trees and parks, but this was the older part of the city and as my mother never failed to tell me, we were lucky to be here. My father I was told repeatedly had left us with nothing. Of course, he hadn't planned to die; who does, at 38? But the fact was we were charity cases thrown on my grandparents' doorstep by fate and dependent on them for support.

I suppose I might have felt differently about Shabbat had my parents been religious, but they didn't even belong to a synagogue, and my father was openly contemptuous of what he chose to call superstition. And while no one ever said anything about it directly, the idea that his illness and eventual death were somehow related to his lack of faith wasn't denied either. It was just out there, a possibility. I didn't know what I believed but having been through a major dislocation it struck me as stupid at the least to deny God's existence, so I trod the path of my maternal grandparents without complaint. I went to school, studied as hard as I needed to, and suffered Saturdays silently. Things could have been worse. I knew that now.

And yet, all this was about to change in dramatic ways and in the process alter the way I saw the world forever. Because no one in our house was allowed to function on the Sabbath and since in my grandfather's world this extended to ordinary household tasks such as turning on the oven or switching the lights on and off, an elderly man had for years been employed at the rate of $.50 an hour to come into our home and perform these chores. Such *shabbos goys* were not unheard of in the larger Jewish community but they were unusual in our neighborhood, so when Herman Kleinschmidt dropped dead of a heart attack, there was some concern about finding someone to take his place.

I was only vaguely aware of this at the time, though I remember hearing whispered conversations between my mother and her parents, which included the word "polska." This was explained the next Saturday when the door opened and a small blonde girl of about my age entered our home. She bowed to my grandfather and then apparently as a result of a prior agreement, turned on the stove and adjusted the thermostat. Before leaving, she looked shyly in my direction, though whether her look expressed good humor or pity I couldn't say. It didn't matter. I was in love.

The girl was not unknown to me, though we'd never spoken. I even knew her name—Sonia Michulka. Nor was she really Polish, or at least I didn't think she was. She and her brother Peter had been introduced as new students at an assembly in school where the principal referred obliquely to the "recent troubles in Europe."

No one in our school knew about Hungarian freedom fighters, though the Jewish kids had been drilled to exhaustion in details of the Holocaust. Hungary was a different matter. If we thought at all about what was then called "The Iron Curtain," it was in a concrete way, as in a limitless extension of steel starting somewhere south of Finland and stretching down over Europe from the Baltic to Trieste. But these were just names and had little to do with the vision who now stood before me.

What was most striking about Sonia from the beginning was that wave of blonde hair and cerulean eyes. That and what I perceived to be her inaccessibility, the impossibility of starting a simple conversation with her about, say, Elvis, or what she might be doing over the weekend. Her brother was reputed to be a gifted pianist though we weren't completely clear as to what that might mean. Jerry Lee Lewis played the piano but looking at Peter with his thick black glasses and delicate fingers, I had the feeling he had little in common with the rock star and probably didn't stand with one foot on the piano as he played.

Sonia was just there that morning in her flounced skirt, smiling anxiously, hands clasped behind her back as the principal spoke of the horrors she'd lived through. She did not look tortured to me. She was just a pretty girl, though in some way a bit off, not the one you'd be likely to pick up at a school dance or meet at the Dairy Queen. She wasn't part of my world, and I had other things on my mind.

If I had not noticed Sonia before, however, I now thought of little else in my waking hours and my sleep was filled with tortured visions of her in provocative poses that more than once led to stained bed sheets I took pains to hide from my mother. I knew without anyone saying anything that in the eyes of my family, she was not for me. If I were to show any overt interest in her, my grandfather would discharge her immediately, so intense was his concern about inter-marriage between Jews and gentiles. As a result, on those Saturdays I allowed myself only the odd furtive glance in Sonia's direction that was in its own way more titillating than a direct examination would have been. The momentary glimpse of a sheaf of pink skin beneath her diaphanous cream blouse, her filigreed underthings barely visible as she bent over to retrieve something, her slightly bowed legs wrapped in brown stockings and the cracked flats she wore even in the dead of winter when snow clogged the streets. I could live on this kind of thing for weeks and did so for fear that any greater display of interest would result in complete ruin. For me, she was both shadow and dream, ethereal yet more real than anything else in my life. She was always with me, though we seldom spoke and only exchanged guilty smiles at the door as she left for the day, making the next seven days until I saw her again an unreasonable penance for I had done nothing to deserve it.

There was a park near our home with a carousel, playground and pond that was heavily used in the summer by families with small children. In the winter the carousel was deserted with only a lonely sign imploring children to "Be Nice" hanging over its entrance, which someone had forgotten to take down. The pond had become a skating rink with one side reserved for the organized brawling of hockey and the other open to skaters of all descriptions. Some turned pirouettes on the ice while others circled the pond serenely, bent over their skates as if they were studying their toes, with arms crossed behind their backs.

Having grown up in Southern California, winter sports were both foreign and exotic to me, so when the few friends I had left on skiing excursions, I would sometimes retreat to the park where I bought hot chocolate at the warming booth and watched the skaters. It was on one of these visits that I saw Sonia, face encircled by a pink ruff with matching mittens, tracing school figures one afternoon near dusk.

She didn't see me at first, occupied as she was in some complicated maneuver that involved backing and spinning in the air, but eventually she noticed me watching and skated over. We had never actually spoken before, but now she was smiling broadly and took me by both hands and shook them. "Well, Dan," she said. Then again, "Mr. Dan, a skater you are too?"

I was going to protest that I had never been on skates in my life and came only for the chocolate but seeing her there in short skirt and tights, the pink ruff accentuating her full red cheeks, I changed my mind. "I'm learning," I said quickly, though the process had yet to begin. "I'm going to take some lessons."

"Ach," she said, and looked me up and down critically. "I'll teach then."

And so it started. I took skating lessons at the pond from Sonia two or three times a week and though I mentioned the identity of my teacher to no one, my enthusiasm was obvious and my family approved. "You've got some color," my grandfather said when I returned one night. And the next week I found a new pair of skates in my room without my having asked for them.

Often in the afternoon, rather than going home after school, I would trail down Federal Boulevard past the 5&10, the newsstand and grocery store, to stop in at my grandfather's clothing store where I'd stay until closing time, playing checkers in the back room or talking to the few customers who came in. Then we'd walk back home together, perhaps stopping on the way to buy some licorice.

Given the paucity of his clientele, it was always a mystery to me how my grandfather provided for all of us, but if he felt any anxiety on this account, he never mentioned it. He had originally found work as a custom tailor before the war, but there wasn't much call for tailored clothing in North Denver, so while he had the odd small job, altering a man's pants or letting out a seam in a woman's dress, he had slowly become a haberdasher, selling lines of clothes vastly inferior to those he had once made himself for young Jewish men who worked downtown in the big buildings on 17th Street in the financial district.

"*Schmatte*," he would say disdainfully, fingering the lapels of a jacket hanging in his store. A rag. "But who cares anymore? Still, a man has to live, Daniel."

It was obvious my grandfather regretted the decline in values, but he didn't feel humiliated by the state of things because he'd done nothing to create them, just as he'd had nothing to do with the influx of Mexicans in Denver or the subsequent rise in crime in our neighborhood. He was neither bitter nor angry. He saw things as they were without feeling personally affronted by them. If his business wasn't what it had once been, it was nevertheless enough to provide for his family and that was all that mattered. The store was warm and comfortable on those long winter afternoons and there was a phonograph in the backroom along with a stack of ancient *The Ring* magazines. My grandfather, who wouldn't swat a troublesome fly had an unlikely fascination with boxing and an encyclopedic knowledge of the sport.

"Stanley Ketchell," he'd say. "Now there was a fighter, Daniel. None of these boys today could get in the ring with him. Or Gentleman Jim Corbett. Never see a fighter like that again."

And I, never having heard of Ketchell or Corbett or Jack Johnson or any of the other fighters he mentioned, listened entranced as the air outside turned blue and the streetlights came on in the city. On one or two magic nights we ventured further into Denver, visiting the Auditorium to see local fighters compete, but my grandfather seemed to prefer talking about the long-ago artists he remembered from his youth to seeing anyone who might actually be competing today.

What I'm trying to suggest here is that my grandfather was a *hamish* guy, comfortable with the way his life had gone, not big on regrets, and accepting of others and the world in general. I came to feel this was a gift, something worth learning about life, though I wasn't very successful at doing so myself.

I was never going to be much of a skater. I had weak ankles and tended to lean so far forward out of fear of falling that I could never work up much momentum on the ice. Double axles and camels were out of the question; staying on my feet was my goal. Sonia must have known this, but she was wonderfully patient and my lessons allowed me to be near her, which made this otherwise frustrating experience something to look forward to.

The pond was long and thin and lit around the warming shack, but at the other end of the ice there was less illumination and as a result fewer skaters. It became my goal to lure Sonia down there, especially since I had noticed there was another much smaller equipment shack that I wanted to investigate. Sonia was more cautious, however. "What if someone sees us?" she asked.

"Then they will," I responded with more bravado than I really felt. "What's wrong with exploring?"

"Oh, Dan, you are so brave," Sonia said, laughing.

But she followed, skating circles around me as I made my dogged way down the ice. The equipment shack was unlocked and though there were some boards and signs inside, there was room for us to slip in as well and I was surprised and pleased by Sonia's willingness to do so. In the close darkness of that little room, we held each other for the first time, trembling from excitement and the cold as my hands tentatively explored her body, first her breasts, then her hips and legs. All the while she laughed softly in my ear and I imagined it was out of pleasure.

When we kissed, I was again surprised both by her eagerness and skill as her tongue explored my mouth expertly, bringing me alive in ways I hadn't known before. My previous experience consisted of kissing games like "Post Office" and "Seven Minutes in Heaven" and there had been few enough of those. But fortunately, in this case sophistication didn't seem to be called for, at least on my part.

"Oh, Dan," Sonia said, and reached down to take me out of my pants. "You are strong. Very strong." I had never heard an erection spoken of in this way before, but it filled me with unreasonable pride even though under her prodding the moment was almost instantly over leaving in its wake a disconsolate feeling of failure. Sonia patted my crotch and kissed me lightly on the cheek and then she was gone, out the door and skating back toward the lighted area as I labored to put myself back together.

That was what winter was like that year. We would meet once or twice a week, skate for a while and then visit the equipment house where we would fondle each other, more for my satisfaction than hers, though I became more skilled as time went on. Other than that, we didn't really see each other. At school, she would pass by with a covey of girls and wave gaily in my direction and of course on Saturdays she came to our house. I believe I was an important but hidden part of her life and in time I came to wonder if this was for my convenience or hers. Was it that she was ashamed of me, and didn't want her friends and family to know about our relationship even as I was hiding it from my family? I never knew but when big school events, a prom or holiday dance came up, I didn't ask Sonia and she never mentioned it. The ice-skating pond in the park represented our private envelope of intimacy and there seemed to be a shared sense that if it were opened or shared with others whatever was inside would vanish immediately.

What did I know of her or she of me? Nothing really, yet it seemed more than enough. And while our trysts at the skating pond had a sexual focus, I would have said my attraction to Sonia had more to do with charm and mystery. With her in that dark booth, surrounded by parking signs and machinery, I felt like a man of the world. She had given me that and I was grateful.

I traveled then in a kind of cocoon, largely unaware of others. I went to school, returned home, had my skating lessons, and experimented with passion. But I floated unthinking in the midst of everything else. So I was only mildly surprised one afternoon to find another older man working the sewing machine at the back of my grandfather's shop. "This is Mr. Michulka," my grandfather said, introducing us. "You know his children already. Sonia comes to us on Shabbos."

Sonia's father stood, tall with stooped shoulders in the cramped space, and shook both my hands. "Yes, yes," he said. "My Sonia's friend, her good friend." In the dark room I thought he might have winked, but I couldn't be sure.

My grandfather didn't respond to this, though it wouldn't have surprised me if he knew the truth about my skating lessons. He didn't miss much that went on around him. Now, however, he just nodded and guided me to the front counter. "A brilliant man," he said, nodding toward the back. "A chemist in the old country, a Ph.D. Here, he can't find work." He shrugged expressively. "*Zoll nicht treffen, vus kin treffen.*" It shouldn't happen, what can happen.

Hiring Mr. Michulka was a generous thing to do, especially given the fact that I seldom saw a customer in my grandfather's store except for the rabbi and cantor of our small synagogue who had their vestments tailored there at what I imagined to be a steep discount. Generous or not, however, it seemed the world was closing in ominously around me. My girlfriend was our shabbos goy and her father was working in my grandfather's shop. What had previously felt like a private obsession was close to becoming an open secret. Accepting as my grandfather was of most things, I knew there would be no genial allowance for that.

Sonia seemed to share none of my anxiety as we sat close to each other in the warming booth the next afternoon, hot chocolate in our gloved hands and the smell of wet wool in the air. Her lips were red and round and asked to be kissed. Her blue eyes wrinkled in mischievous amusement at my discomfort. Had I been more experienced I might have understood that her family had been through worse in their escape from Hungary, that she had experienced real terror in her life. But in that place, at that time, it seemed that nothing could be more disastrous than having our secret love revealed. "Your Papa not like me?" Sonia asked now, smiling again.

She called my grandfather papa, not caring for the distinctions between generations, and it seemed apt since I had no father. I shifted in my seat uncomfortable with the truth. For my grandfather, the most gracious and generous of men, knew everyone in our small neighborhood without having one gentile friend. Did he like or dislike them? For him, I suspected, gentiles did not even exist on that axis. "It's not that," I said.

Sonia nodded. Her blonde ponytail was bound in a small red kerchief. I thought she was inexpressively lovely and, on the spot, began plotting our escape together. "Then what...?"

It was an entirely reasonable question since we had done nothing wrong, save for a few kisses, some transient touching, the casual hug before parting. I knew, of course, this would be more than enough for my family. They would say things always started in such a way and as far as that went they would be right. Without anyone saying so directly, an ancient fear that voicing something made it more likely to occur, what they worried about where I was concerned was intermarriage and as a result the destruction of the race. In their minds this was what had taken my mother away in the first place and probably led to my father's early death and consequent abandonment of us. God works in mysterious ways, the rabbi intoned from the Bima, though it seemed to me that the punishment should fit the crime. "Nothing, " I said now. "Forget it."

Sonia's eyes crossed briefly in puzzlement or irritation. Then she said, "Okay." And as far as I know she did forget it. We went out on the ice again and then to the far reaches of the lagoon, where neither lights nor the other skaters could reach us. She let me lean her against a tree and then run my hands beneath her sweater and cup her breasts. "Oh, Danny," she giggled. "Your hands are cold."

"But my heart is warm," I replied, emboldened by lust.

She laughed and then she reached down to my crotch and palpated my groin. "Not just heart," she said and then she laughed again.

Things happened quickly after that, as if by passing over an imaginary sexual boundary, I had set off some kind of inter-racial signal that could not be ignored. Though how this might have been transmitted to anyone else remained unknown to me.

The next Monday I was summoned to the rabbi's study for a talk. He was an old man with an accent so thick I had trouble understanding him. He radiated solemnity and the legend was that he had spent time in a concentration camp, though he could have avoided it because he had chances to leave Galicia. He insisted on waiting until all his flock had left and in the end it turned out he waited too long.

My grandfather sat silently in the corner as the rabbi spoke softly about the evils of interfaith dating. No one mentioned Sonia but when my grandfather and I walked home afterwards there was no stop at the candy store for licorice.

The following Saturday, it was not Sonia but her father who appeared at our house to adjust the range and thermostat and when I went to the park with my skates, she didn't appear, though I waited and scanned the horizon hopefully with each new arrival.

We never spoke again. If I saw her in the hall at school, she would wiggle her fingers in greeting and then giggle with her friends. I can't say I was broken-hearted, however. The truth was I was grateful to Sonia for having, if only briefly, raised the shroud in which I had been living, for allowing me to breathe and laugh again. I couldn't really say she had been my girlfriend, that we had had what in the future I would call a relationship. But we had known each other intimately and intimacy is always valuable.

Over time, she came to seem less real and more ephemeral, especially once high school was over and we went different ways. In fact, in years to come I wondered fancifully if she could have been a *dybbuk*, an apparition, though one with no evil intentions, and that I had imagined everything, from her blonde presence in our home, to the fleeting touch of her lips and the round warmth of her breasts in a dark place on a cold winter night.

LOCKED AND LOADED

He shouldn't have had a gun. Ben Rathburn. In saying that, I don't mean guns should be outlawed, though this might be true. But that's beside the point. Guns are a reality in our neighborhood. We are heavily armed just the same, locked and loaded, ready at all times for anyone foolish enough to invade Greengate and defile our quiet streets and spacious yards. Small explosions disturb our evenings at regular intervals, fireworks lighting up the cloudy night sky or someone taking target practice in his backyard. No one even notices or mentions it anymore. I'm not talking about that. Ben Rathburn, specifically, shouldn't have had a gun and yet he did, and that's where this story starts and ends.

People had talked about the Rathburns since they moved into the old McCloskey place fifteen years before all this happened. I call it the McCloskey place even though they were only around for five years or so. No one knows who was in that house before that. We're a relatively young community; we don't have long memories. McCloskey was an assistant coach with the Broncos and liked to throw his money around. Consequently, his house was larger than the others on the block with ornate statues in front and the kind of half-timber siding my mother used to call "fake English cottage style." The house was really too big for such a small family, and the talk was that the Rathburns would likely have more kids, but time went by, and no other siblings came along to keep Ben company. He was in grade school then, a tow-headed boy who smiled a lot as he rode his bike around our block. He did odd jobs like raking leaves or shoveling snow in winter though he never did anything like this for us.

His parents were named Miles and Ruby and though I didn't know them well we were friendly as was common in the Village. We'd talk if we ran into each other on the street. Ruby was a pretty brunette who wore short skirts and blew kisses when I'd see her walking in the Arboretum. I once asked Miles how they were and he said Ruby gave the best blowjobs of any of the Tri Delts at Northwestern. He may have meant to shock me and he did. People in Greengate seldom talked openly about sex and this seemed like an odd thing to say at a garden party. It also seemed a little disrespectful to his wife, but people have gotten married for worse reasons.

As a follow-up, I asked Miles what he did for a living. "Not much," he said, which is the kind of thing you say if you don't want to get into it. "I've got a law degree, but I've never practiced."

I knew he rented space in the office building near the jail where many lawyers rented, so I said, "But you've got an office."

Miles smirked. "You're a man, you've got to have an office, right? I go there to read my mail, check the internet, sleep with my secretary, you know."

He talked as if we were men of the world, sharing confidences, but I had never thought of work this way, had no office myself and immediately felt inadequate, as if I'd neglected something. When I repeated the conversation to my wife, however, she cut to the heart of the matter immediately. "I smell a trust fund," she said simply.

I had to admit she didn't seem wrong in this, though it hadn't occurred to me. Ruby didn't work; they had an elegant home too big for their small family and drove expensive cars. What were the possibilities? Ruby also took pictures, though not professionally, and she often posted idyllic shots of the family running down sand dunes or vacationing in the mountains. An ideal life, or so it seemed, even if Ruby described Greengate disdainfully as "the bubble," far outside what might be truly hip and interesting to her. We were given to believe that people as interesting as the Rathburns were only blessing us with their presence for Ben's sake, because of the good schools and clean air.

Ironically, it was the very fact of Greengate's removal from city life that drew most of us here, whatever Ruby might have thought of it. When I lived in New York, I loved the energy that seemed to drift up from the sidewalks, along with the ripe smell of garbage and dogshit. I liked the rumble of the subway underway, the nearly constant racket from trucks, steam shovels, buses, and people yelling at one another, on the street and in hallways. I liked the crowding, the rough contact of others in close spaces, the smell of tobacco, perfume and shoe leather along with wet wool in the winter. I liked the smell of fresh-mown grass in Madison Square Park, and I liked seeing the bums who'd slept on the benches in the park and were just waking up when I went by. My mother said that when I was a baby the only way she could get me to sleep was to walk me in my carriage around the streets near our walk-up on Second Avenue. All of that was as natural as blood in my veins.

Though it might seem odd nothing had really changed for me living in the suburbs. In the quiet shush-shushing of trees overhead, and the occasional roar of cars three or four streets away, there was always a city rhythm in the background. If I closed my eyes, I could still imagine the crosstown buses running past my door, the hum of the underground traffic, heard but not seen. We all came to Greengate for the silence after noisy lives in the city, but for me at least it was an active silence. Even inside my house, I could always hear the mail truck as it went down the block, the boy next door screeching away from the curb with his girlfriend, the little kids playing down the street and there was always a slight susurrus in my ears, rather than the total absence of sound, as if someone had unpacked a box of cotton in my head. An unquiet silence, maybe, but not unwelcome.

Provocative as Ruby's comments about our "bubble" might have been, people in Greengate mostly go their own way and let others do the same. Though Miles had said he didn't work, increasingly he was gone for longer periods of time doing something out of town. Ruby came to the neighborhood Christmas party and flirted with other men, carrying a bough of mistletoe around with her and kissing everyone. Though she was young and pretty, she began to seem a bit strained as she moved into her late thirties and forties. Given her husband's habits, I thought of her as something of a grass widow, but I wasn't concerned or sympathetic enough to approach and ask how she was or what was going on with them. Then in the moment, I might have suspected something serious was amiss between them, Miles would suddenly appear, and things would go back to whatever was normal.

Time went by, Ben grew into adolescence, Miles and Ruby carried on as they had and for me life rotated away from the Rathburns. I had almost no contact with them on a daily basis for months at a time until one morning I got a call from Ruby who sounded panicky and asked to speak to my wife. This was out of the ordinary since my wife had even less to do with the neighbors than I did, considering them all accidental fragments of her life. Still, she took the phone, and I immediately recognized her doctor's identity taking over.

"What's going on?" she asked, then listened attentively, making notes every so often.

I wasn't in on the conversation, but I heard her mention a hospital and the names of a couple of other doctors. Was Ruby ill, I wondered? Or Miles. But it turned out it was Ben, sixteen by this time, who'd been arrested for drunk driving on Colorado Boulevard. I hadn't even known he was old enough to drive but kids grow up and do stupid things. It wasn't out of the ordinary in my experience. When my wife hung up, I asked what the matter was, and she told me.

"So now you're their doctor?"

"God no," she said. "I just gave them a few names of people they could call. I guess he'll be all right. If it was drugs, I might feel differently."

But this wasn't the end of it. My wife may have thought she wasn't Ben's doctor, but Ruby acted as if she was on retainer, calling frequently to ask questions about child development, then coming around and standing on one foot on our porch grinning widely and asking if the doctor was in. When my wife brought her into the front room and closed the door for a quiet chat, I wondered if things had changed.

"So now she's your new best friend?"

"Right," my wife said. "I had to talk to her, that's all."

"Why?"

She shrugged. "I'm a doctor. I feel a responsibility whether I like it or not. The Hippocratic Oath."

Who understands people, even those you live with? For years, my wife had kept her distance from our neighbors, avoiding parties and not engaging people on the street unless there was no choice. Somehow Ruby had broken through her reserve and despite what she had said about her responsibility as a doctor, I wondered if there was more to it than that. I had asked but after what she had said, I didn't want to push further. We didn't have that kind of relationship. A large part of our happy marriage had to do with leaving the other person alone if that was what she wanted.

Things got more complicated a few years later. We were at a birthday party when Ruby took my wife into the next room and confided that she and Miles were having marital problems. This wasn't a surprise to me given Miles' long absences from home, but now Ruby was trying to supplement the professional help they were getting. She said she didn't like their marriage therapist, felt she was siding with Miles, and wanted my wife's advice. Following this, she checked in regularly to tell my wife the latest outrageous interpretation the therapist had made. "So unfair," I heard Ruby say more than once. "So so unfair."

I could see my wife regretted having opened herself to Ruby in the first place but having done so she was in for it now and really had no one to blame but herself. "I can put her off when she calls," I suggested. "Save you the headache."

But my wife just shook her head. "I really can't do that," she said. "Avoid her."

"But you're not a marriage therapist," I said.

"I don't know any I could recommend," my wife said.

"So there you are, off the hook, right?"

My wife smiled tolerantly. "That's not how it works," she said.

It is interesting what you find out about people, even people you know intimately, when you're not trying. I had always seen my wife, tall and elegant, standing apart not only from neighbors but from most other people and because of that believed that I had somehow qualified for inclusion in a very small but exclusive club without knowing exactly how I'd gotten here. Now Ruby, whom I thought of as the antithesis of anything approaching elegance, had broken through the gossamer net and was regularly taking up residence in our parlor for long, private chats. I was more curious than jealous, but this was unique, and I wondered what would come of it, especially since I was privy to no tidbits of gossip. Though my wife continued to insist Ruby wasn't a patient, she took doctor/patient confidentiality seriously.

They made an odd couple, Ruby short and bouncy with black hair and bright red lipstick and my wife, austere in gray and black, sitting bent over nodding her head as if in tune to some unheard rhythm. What would come of this, I wondered. And did it make friendship with Miles in some way incumbent upon me? God only knew what other insights he'd offer into fraternity life at Northwestern. This turned out to be unnecessary as the conferences grew fewer and far between after a month or so and we returned to our previous pattern without interruptions from Ruby, though I wondered if they would recur sometime in the future when a new family crisis presented itself.

Greengate prides itself on its "mature vegetation" in contrast to the other newer and more expensive communities sprouting up to our south and west but the tall trees that cover our streets also sometimes serve as baffles for whatever conflict may erupt at a given time in one home or another. A screaming wife who discovers her adulterous husband or teenagers slamming doors as they escape from one family uprising or another, the noises from a backyard party that's out of hand and then the predictable yelling and cheering at the backyard hockey games bordering our backyard on the odd Thursday night in January. After any or all of this, we retreat into our homes, visible only by the blue light of television at a window or from the telltale line of smoke from a chimney or backyard barbecue. People in Greengate make a fetish of remaining uninvolved in the affairs of others which is not the same as uninterest. If someone wants to talk, we're always there, perhaps sympathetic, but that's as far as it goes. Even at parties, no one asks a question that might by the wildest guess be considered personal or political and yet we're always listening, ear to the ground for a tremor in someone else's world.

Thus, it was that time went by with news of other children moving on, graduating from high school or college and then, finally, getting married, raising the possibility of grandchildren appearing in Greengate to start the progression again. New families moved in, people died, Greengate replicated itself. And in time, word came that young Ben Rathburn had gone off to a small college in Indiana, a religious school someone thought, even if the Rathburns didn't seem particularly religious.

Ben came back wearing his school sweatshirt, a bumper sticker went on Miles' sedan and then abruptly it seemed the wheels came off. When I saw Ruby at the grocery store, she informed me that Ben was taking a year off from college, though he'd been only been there one semester.

"He's always loved languages," Ruby said bobbing her head in affirmation and adding "you know," as if this must be common knowledge. "So, he's going to Germany."

I showed what I considered to be appropriate interest and happened to mention my time there in the service which made Ruby shake her head irritably. "Not Frankfort," she said. "Too fucking boring. He's going to Heidelberg."

"Ah," I said. "A scholar," as if I'd been familiar with the work of Heidegger and others of the Heidelberg royalty.

"Right," Ruby said. "All those guys." Then she was gone.

It was hard to know how Ben did in the great European university since he was back in the neighborhood barely three months later with the simple explanation that he liked Italy better than Germany, but he got drunk at the neighborhood Oktoberfest celebration anyway. Ruby had her arm around him and told everyone how good it was to "have my boy back home." If Ben was moved by this, he didn't show it and kept saying "Sehr Gut" to all who would listen as if to attest to his study in Deutschland. He was twenty by this time and had grown tall and broad with the suggestion of a beer gut being a visible reminder of his time in Europe. When he sauntered up to me, I asked how he'd liked the famous German university during his time there.

Ben grimaced. "Like it was okay, man, but really old. I mean really, you know. And I'm not that into studying."

I wasn't sure why you'd go to Heidelberg otherwise but nodded just the same as if what he'd said was the most reasonable thing in the world. The party moved around us, men holding their drinks high over their heads, women clustered together, drunken laughter emitting from the groups sporadically. I had thought I was done with Ben, but he didn't move and in fact seemed to sway back and forth to some mysterious melody in his head. We were standing close together and I felt an obligation to carry on a conversation with this boy. "Going back to Indiana then?" I asked. I couldn't remember the name of his school.

Ben was looking around and over my shoulder so may not have heard the question. "Hey, maybe," he said. "We'll see."

"Something else planned instead?" I asked. He had said he didn't like studying.

"Maybe I'll join the Marines," he said. "Like go to Afghanistan or something. I want to see the war for myself, don't trust the lamestream media to tell us anything, you know?"

This was interesting and new, even a bit provocative pushing back at the media. I knew Miles was a Republican, but Ben had never shown any interest in politics as far as I knew. "The Marines?" I said. "See the world. How did you decide on that?"

"Were you in the service?" he asked, showing the slightest glimmer of interested.

"Army, " I said. "I got drafted."

"Army's for pussies," Ben said. "Marines are tough sonsabitches."

Which must have been how Ben saw himself, a leatherneck ready for battle, which seemed bizarre standing in the backyard with drinks in our hands, but people are allowed to have their own fantasies about themselves. "Have fun at Parris Island," I said.

"Yeah," Ben said, as if he'd never heard of the place. Then he moved away, throwing "See you later" over his shoulder as he went.

As it turned out, however, Ben quit the Indiana school for good and washed out of the Marines in six weeks after which he returned to Greengate. There was a brief hiatus during which he joined a right-wing demonstration in Michigan and then, we were told, spent a few weeks at a militia training camp in Washington state. Ruby told me he was trying to finish his degree online but in a rare display of candor, she remarked in an offhand way, "That kid's pretty fucked up is the truth. That's his fulltime job right now."

If this seemed a harsh way to talk about one's own child, Ruby might be excused since she was going through a tough time herself and moved out of the family home in the dead of night a couple of weeks after we spoke. Word filtered back to Greengate that she was living with a man ten years younger than she in the Golden Triangle near the art museum, having apparently at last made it to an area more interesting than Greengate. No one liked Miles much but there was general sympathy for a man whose wife had moved out leaving him with a teen-aged boy with problems. And given my few interactions with him, I was impressed that Miles had stepped up, whatever his reasons for doing so might be.

Having viewed all this from a distance, which is always my preference, I was brought into the frame when we got a call from Miles later in the week. I had hardly spoken to him in years, so this was a surprise, but it turned out that he, like Ruby, really wanted to talk to my wife. After a short conversation, she hung up and said, "We've got to go over there."

"Why me?" I asked. "He called you."

"I'm not going over there by myself," my wife said. "It sounds like that kid's psychotic."

"I thought what you usually did in situations like that was call the cops and have him taken to the hospital."

"They called me," my wife said. "I'm a doctor. You'd only call the police if he was a danger to himself or someone else."

"He's not? Then why did Miles call?"

"Let's go," my wife said.

There was no point in arguing so we went over to Miles' house to see Ben. When Miles opened the door, we could see that someone had trashed the living room before we arrived. Chairs were up turned, paintings were off the wall, and there was a large hole in the center of the tv screen mounted on the wall.

"Thanks for coming," Miles said. "He's in there."

We walked toward the bedroom he'd indicated but at the door, Ben screamed, "Not you, goddamnit. Just her."

I backed off and whispered to my wife, "I'm right here if you need me."

She nodded and entered the room. Miles and I stood in the hallway looking at each other but there wasn't really anything to say. Everything was quiet in the bedroom, but we could hear whispering and then after a few moments, Ben sobbing loudly. I looked at Miles and he shrugged as if to say this represented progress. After fifteen minutes, my wife emerged holding a pill bottle.

"Who gave him this much Haldol?" she asked.

"It was a doctor in the hospital," Miles said, naming a mental hospital in the center of town.

"What was he doing there?"

"Ruby had him committed before she left," Miles said. "They let him out after two days."

"Because they had to," my wife said. "With this much Haldol on board, though, I'm surprised he can stand upright. I'm going to cut the dose in half and call a doctor I know that might have time." She put her hand on Miles' shoulder. "I'm sorry," she said, "but Ben's really sick. He should be in day hospital at least."

"Can't you see him instead?" Miles said.

"No," my wife said simply. "I'm a neighbor, I can't be his doctor." Miles didn't object to this but that didn't stop him from calling several more times during the next week even if he'd been able to get Ben an appointment with the doctor my wife had mentioned.

"Why do you keep taking his calls?" I said. "Why is it your problem?"

"It's not," my wife said. "But I feel responsible until I get someone to see this boy or get him in the hospital. The guy's wife just left him alone with this crazy kid to try to take care of."

I couldn't disagree with this. As far as I'm concerned, character is all about doing the hard things you don't have to do. I knew I wouldn't have done what my wife had and I admired her for it. Fortunately, things seemed to calm down after this. First, Ben stayed in another hospital for a few days and got his medications adjusted. Then Ruby called to thank my wife and say Ben was staying with her and was now much better. Miles bought Ben a new truck to drive back and forth and the hope was that Ruby might be right this time. The next week, Miles put his house on the market and when it sold immediately, I assumed that soon we would have seen the last of the Rathburns. That would have provided a conclusion, a mystifying exit after which nothing would be heard of the family again, a neat ending to a neighborhood saga, but of course that isn't what happened. Life is seldom neat or well-organized.

How can anyone know what young Ben Rathburn was thinking or feeling out on the highway that night in the middle of a winter squall, the snow tearing his eyes, the red taillights of cars speeding past blurred in his vision along with the blue lights of a police cruiser and the accompanying siren's deafening scream. Did Ben know it was three am or where he was? Did he wonder where his ride had gone, why he was no longer in the warm car with the radio cushioning his thoughts or imagine that he'd somehow landed in the middle of a kaleidoscopic light show, if he was at a rave perhaps, and that the noise punishing his ears was the band warming up? Who can know if in the uproar he heard the cops' shouted warnings for what they were or in his delirium imagined it was his high school track coach yelling at him to run faster? Maybe in his fantasy he thought it was his old drill instructor from the Marines three inches from his ear screaming for all he was worth. And if Ben did, as the news reports said, pull the assault rifle out of the canvas carrying bag and then point it in the direction of the cops who'd been called by the kid who brought him to the Happy Canyon turnoff and then drove away, allegedly because Ben had scared him with the gun in his bag, if he did point the gun, it's anyone's guess if Ben would actually have tried to kill the troopers and not merely hold the AR-15 up for their inspection. He might have been proud of this latest acquisition; might have thought it would go well in the back window of the pickup Miles had bought him. But at this point it's too late to know anything and perhaps pointless even to wonder how a sweet kid from down the block could have been shot and left to die on the side of the road at the age of twenty-three in a battle with state cops on a windy highway in the dead of winter.

The papers didn't call it a tragedy but then they didn't know Ben or his parents or what they'd all been through lately. Would things have been different if the cops had merely tazed Ben rather than shooting or if going off his prescription the week before hadn't made him psychotic? It's too late to know any of that or indeed to know anything except that this shouldn't have happened because Ben Rathburn should never have had that gun.

THE AUTHOR

David Milofsky is an award-winning author with seven published novels and a previous collection of short fiction. His most recent novel was *Scare Tactics* (Serving House, 2025). He has received fellowships for his work from Breadloaf, the MacDowell Colony, and the National Endowment for the Arts. Milofsky served as editor of *Denver Quarterly* and *Colorado Review* and was the founding editor of the Colorado Prize in Poetry. An Emeritus Professor of English at Colorado State University, he lives in Colorado with his wife Jean.